I CALL HIM HIM

Scott W. Kimak

CONTENTS

The Message

"Hey, pencil-neck," Bill said, as they traveled the worn path and came in sight of Madisonville. "You have a hole in your shoe so big even my enormous tongue would fit into it."

"You know, you can really be disgusting," I replied. "I don't know why the big guy keeps you around."

"He loves me. He just doesn't know it yet," Bill replied. "One of these days I'm going to get him to crack a smile."

"Good luck with that," I said as I noticed HIM's eyes fixated straight ahead, cold and unblinking. Did HE even hear us? In all these years, I had never seen him smile, cry, or even laugh. He knows we are here, but it is rare that he ever recognizes us, and when he does, all we usually get is just a nod from his head. What was behind that dark stare?

I call him – HIM, for I do not know his name. However, is he truly a man? Can a man be utterly devoid of emotion? Can he be lost in darkness with only the focus of revenge to push him forever forward? We have traveled together for many years, and during this time, I have questioned his reality. I have never seen him sleep. I have never seen him eat. I've never even seen him take a bowel movement.

It's not just my eyes that have been blind to his existence. My ears have never heard him speak or make any sound whatsoever. Riding at his side, I can definitely smell his horse, yet the rider leaves no stench good or bad that I can recognize.

All these things have puzzled me during our travels, but what puzzles me most is his uncanny movement in battle. No human being can move as fast as I've seen him move. I've watched him cut through a host of demons in the blink of an eye with as much effort as it takes me to brush my teeth.

Many times, I've wondered if he is real or some mythical creature possessed with superpowers. If you can believe the old stories, then it is said that he once was a human long ago, before the Last War. However, that war changed everything, and what came after transformed HIM into whatever he is now.

I leave this journal, so people in the future won't forget what our world once was. I've already lost much of what I learned about the old days before the Last War. What I do know is that man reached a point where he felt he could question God. Yes, I will say his name regardless of the consequences if I am discovered. For in this time, God does not exist, and it is certain torture and death to speak his name. However, before the War, many still believed in him and professed their faith freely. Regardless, the majority started doubting whether God existed and strived to become Gods themselves. If the stories are true, then it is hard to doubt they succeeded, for it was a time of miracles.

It is said that man could cast his voice from one village to the next, the sound traveling for miles through tiny wires. And he created armor wagons that could float into the sky or move across the deserts ten times faster than a horse could run.

There were many miracles during this time, both good and bad. One of these was said to prevent war with the threat of war. This creation was the masterpiece of man, but it was also his doom. He created thousands of objects that looked like giant swords. They could travel through the air for many miles, landing in villages and setting them ablaze. During the Last War, the armies of men launched all these swords into the air and started a fire that burned the entire planet to dust. Almost every man, woman, and child died that day.

Some survivors, including HIM, hid deep underground and lived in relative peace for many years. Unfortunately, when these last humans decided to venture to the surface and try to rebuild, they encountered something beyond fixing. They assumed nothing remained after the apocalypse, but they were sorely mistaken. What survived wasn't human, and any semblance of God was gone. A shadow of evil now controlled the earth, and they were hell-bent on exterminating any humans who still lived.

That was when I entered the story, --- almost five years ago. It was right after they butchered my dark companion's wife and daughter, sending him forth on his destructive path of darkness.

Unfortunately, I never had the honor of meeting his family, but others say his wife balanced strength and beauty like no other woman. They say she was small and lithe but could back down people twice her size with her quick wit and fierce independence. With the roar of a tiger, she protected that little cub daughter of hers but also with uncompromising love.

His daughter was said to be a princess on the rise, blessed with a regal bearing, commanding respect from anyone she met. Kindness came naturally to her, but she was her mother's daughter, and pity the fool who confused this with naivety. She was gorgeous and could have led just in beauty alone, as every young boy chased after her, and every old man wished he was young enough to be with her. To top this off, she was brilliant beyond imagination, and many believed she would be the leader who would bring humankind back to greatness one day.

Sometimes for a moment, when I think about his family, I can see why he changed into this dark demi-god of destruction, but then my rational mind pulls me back, and I know I can never be like him. How can someone only be a weapon and not have a conscience anymore? What they did to his family was beyond horrible, but I fear what he has become. Even if he kills them all, what will be the point if he loses his soul? Will he become as dark as Satan himself? What will Bill and I do to stop him if that is where his destiny leads?

That's right, I kind of skimmed by Bill, and you don't really know much about him. Bill joined our little trio exactly one year after the death of our dark friend's family. Our silent companion marks the anniversary on a saddlebag, and that's why I remember it so well. He had just finished marking the bag, and not a second later, Bill just rides into our camp unannounced. It surprised the hell out of me. No one ever sneaks up on us, yet Bill made it seem easy. He cracked some joke about how loud our farts were, and that's why we didn't hear him.

If you haven't figured it out by now, Bill is the comedian of our trio. He drives me crazy most of the time, but at least I can talk with him. I think I would have gone insane if it wasn't for Bill. In the five years that I've traveled with my dark and brooding friend, he hasn't spoken a word. Bill has been my comic relief and the complete opposite of our silent partner.

"Hey, big guy, the village is just over that hill," said Bill. "Doesn't that hill look like a big titty? Maybe it looks that way because I haven't been laid forever. What do you think, Mr. Rational?"

"I think you have no manners," I replied. Turning toward HIM, I said, "Bill and I will stay at the top of the hill and cover your retreat. Signal us if you need any help."

My dark friend was already moving away, and I don't even know if he heard us. Why do I always ask him if he needs help? Even if he did, he wouldn't ask for it.

For someone who has killed so many, he is not what you would expect at first appearance. He is slightly above average height, with a thatch of light-brown hair, frosted with a tinge of grey. His face has a noble look, with a high forehead and a granite, square chin. His nose was more prominent than most men's, seeming slightly out of proportion; however, it did not lessen his attractiveness. His eyes were narrow, possibly from years of squinting to avoid the dust and ash that churns across the landscape. But if you looked closely into those eyes, you would see the vibrant sparkle of blue and a combination of both sadness and intelligence. You would think that someone of his grim nature would be covered head to toe in scars from his many battles. Surprisingly, the only ones he carried were very small, adorning his left cheek and temple.

The man was dressed entirely in black, and no armor whatsoever covered his body. Instead, his clothes were loose and baggy, meant for speed and flexibility. Sometimes when he moved a certain way, you could see the muscles ripple beneath the cloth, but he wasn't overly muscled. His stature was more like Apollo than Hercules. To finish off his attire, two long swords were strapped on each side of a belt, tied unceremoniously around his waist.

We could see the village below, and it wasn't much different than the hundreds of towns we had seen over the years. That's right; you haven't been with us all this time, so let me indulge you.

Most villages we come across are nothing but rubble, but there have been a few where every structure is left intact. This village was a combination of both. On the east side of the road, several structures were still standing; some of these were even more than one level in height. Broken windows were at every turn. The shards of glass looked like hungry fangs ready to attack. Doors were missing or hanging by a few threads on their hinges. Most roofs were gone, and the ones that remained sagged or twisted inward, like a deformity hoping to escape its misery. In all its awkwardness, at least the east side had a slight essence of its former self. The west side was nothing more than a crumbling mess of chaos. Nothing remained standing. Littered with broken concrete and debris, it was melancholy and deserted of life.

The worst part was the rancid smell. From where we stood, it must have been close to a hundred yards to the village, yet I needed to cover my face as I felt the compulsion to vomit. Glancing at Bill, I saw he was in the same predicament, hanging over his horse and dry heaving like a rat had crawled down his throat. Yet my dark friend didn't seem bothered in the least by the toxic smell. With only the purpose of death on his mind, he continued trotting forward, emotionless.

At this point, the dark shapes started to slither out from the structures to the east. First, it was only one figure, but then several more appeared. They were as black as the night sky, shuffling about with that dead look on their faces, but demons aren't dead. I know this because I've seen them up close. They breathe, they think, and best of all, they bleed. They may not seem alive like we are, but they live, fed by the call to evil.

The creatures come in all sizes. Some a full head taller than myself and others as short as a young child. However, this seems to be the only difference. Every single one we've encountered is hairless from head to toe; even the eyebrows are missing. Their eyes are dull and lifeless, almost zombie-like. If I didn't know any better, I would think they were blind. Their dark skin is shriveled, covered with open sores, oozing pus in a never-ending stream of decay, covering gaunt, emaciated bodies.

They appear to be more human than animal, and their actions make me believe this is true. Of all the species on this planet, only man tortures others, and these black soulless creatures are experts in this area. Time after time, I have seen them torture survivors like us in their sadistic rituals, cutting flesh little by little, all the while screaming fanatically in praise to their dark master. However, this time they seemed to be alone.

As my dark friend approached, they stepped back, letting him enter their ranks. They closed in and surrounded him, but caution held them from attack. My friend's reputation had grown over the years, and even demons could now feel fear from

HIM.

"You may pass. Our master is waiting for you at Hus – town," spoke the lead demon in its gurgled, black speech.

My friend, as usual, made no response. He sat steadily on his mount with no indication that he had even heard the monstrosity speak.

In a frustrated tone, the lead demon raised its voice and said, "You may leave. We will not attack you!"

Once again, no response from my dark friend. What the demon didn't realize was that it didn't matter if they attacked or not. They were already dead, and there was nothing they could do to stop it from happening.

"Bring out the popcorn. The show is about to start," said Bill with his usual chuckle. "I'll bet you a brewsky that you can't see his blades move."

"I'll take that bet," I responded with a smile.

The lead demon was infuriated over the disrespect it received in not being acknowledged, shaking its arms, and stomping its feet. The creature took a quick step forward and pointed its spear toward HIM. It was the last thing the monster ever did, and I wonder if it even had time to understand its mistake. I told you earlier how uncanny the speed of my friend was. For years Bill and I had made a bet on which one of us would be first to see his swords move. So far, we hadn't had much luck, and it didn't look like tonight would be any better. Our friend had already jumped off his horse, flipped through the air, and removed the lead demon's head before it ever lifted its spear above its shoulders. Crimson mist sprayed in every direction, and panic broke out. Some demons, foolish or brave, came forward; others ran for their lives.

Bill and I watched from the top of the hill, as we had so many times in the past. Every time we saw him move, our admiration grew for our dark companion. Once again, his blades moved beyond what a human eye can catch, and sometimes his entire body was lost from our view. Upward swings removed arms, and thrusts were in and out so fast that blood didn't find time to drip before the next victim fell. One of the demons swung his club high, but my friend dropped low and swept his legs out. Before the creature could hit the ground, an upward swing divided its body in half. Within seconds, seven demons were dead, and only one remained. This was the first monster that had tried to run. The creature was nearly a hundred feet away, but it wouldn't be far enough. Pulling a blade from his sleeve, our dark friend sent a perfect throw right into the back of this unfortunate creature's head.

Some people might find our watching these events gruesome or without empathy. If you had seen the atrocities these vile creatures performed on our people, I assure you that you would think differently. Death was the only thing these abominations deserved, and our dark companion was judge, jury, and executioner.

Without a word, our dark friend mounted his horse and moved forward as if nothing had just occurred. Bill and I spurred our mounts into a gallop to catch up with him.

"Well, that went as expected," said Bill with a sly smile on his face. "I guess you owe me a brewsky."

"Yeah, you can put it on my tab," I responded as I furrowed my eyebrows.

"What's bugging you, pinhead?"

"What the demon said about his master waiting for us in Hus - town,"

"That's your problem. You always overanalyze everything. It's a freaking demon. You can't believe anything they say."

Maybe Bill was right, but if so, then why was my gut telling me something else. This was the first time in five years that the demons had acted this way. Usually, they either attacked immediately or worked themselves into a frenzy and then charged forward. This was the first time they didn't want to fight. It was the first time the creatures tried to have a conversation with our friend. In past encounters, the only dialogue was obscenities and vile gestures. What had changed, and who was this master they claimed was in Hus - town?

Legend had it that Hus - town was once a great village about one hundred miles to the south. I won't believe it until I see it, but the elders say some structures still stand, reaching up into the dark clouds. Supposedly, more than a million people lived in this village before the Last War and miracles proliferated everywhere.

It's said that each day people traveled back and forth inside long, steel snakes. Why the snakes wouldn't eat them, I cannot fathom. Every person owned a steel wagon controlled by magic. Unbelievably, it could move without a horse pulling it. Finally, let me tell you about the greatest joke that leaves me doubting any of these stories. Some elders say that every person had a magic mirror they kept in their pocket. Supposedly the mirror could answer all questions. Some say it became like a drug, and people couldn't stop looking at it. They didn't look at each other and wandered the streets blindly, transfixed to the mirror in a drunken stupor. Humans had done stupid things in the past, but I doubt they would let a mirror control them.

Another thing that didn't seem right about the demon's story was the mention of a master. The only master they had was Satan himself. We had only seen one leader from each small group in our previous encounters, but we had never heard of any type of organized hierarchy. Was there actually a master leader In Hus – town, or did they expect us to believe Satan himself was waiting to meet us? Well, I guess we won't have to wait long to alleviate my anxiety. We should reach Hus – town in a few days.

Angelica

Angelica rested her backside on the broken roof, tucking her slim knees close to her chest. The wind whisked through her thin brown hair, sending strands spiraling in every direction. Her deep majestic-blue eyes stared up into the night sky, just like they had many times in her short ten years of life. Every time she strained her eyes, trying to find the bright stars her parents had told her about, but so far, she had failed to see them. The stars tried to push through the wall of shadow, but they were denied their plea for amnesty, as the dark clouds would not bow to their request. The ominous mist blanketed the sky as it had every day since the Last War ended, so many years ago. The young girl wanted to see these beautiful stars so badly, and every night she prayed to God to make the black mist disappear.

Her parents had taught her to pray to God, but it was a secret, and according to her parents, it was the greatest secret ever. She must pray in silence, for if anyone heard her, then her family would surely die. The demons sometimes took her people as slaves, but if they found you were a believer, then you were sure to be sacrificed.

She had only seen demons once, a year ago. However, before the creatures reached them, she and her parents hid in a sub–basement. The young girl peered through a crack in the concrete as the dark beasts shuffled above her, small pebbles and dust splattering in every direction. She assumed her family was safe, believing the monsters would pass by, but then they spread out and started to search all the standing structures.

Fortunately, Angelica's parents had already prepared for this by creating a ruse to fool the demons. There were several large boxes in the basement corner, standing nearly as tall as her father. The boxes were empty, but at the halfway point, a small ledge was added on the inside that could support the weight of another box, slipped in from the top. Garbage, debris, and any other useless items would fill the top compartment. Without close inspection, it would appear that the entire box was filled, when in actuality, someone in a crouched position could easily hide in the bottom half.

Seeing the demons coming, the young girl's parents bolted to the boxes on padded feet. In one motion, Angelica's father lifted her by the waist, and she slipped her feet inside the cardboard structure. Her mother followed her movement, and the two of them squatted down, clinging to each other with shaking arms. Her father quietly slipped the prepared fake box above them, blocking out any dim light and submerging them in utter darkness. Then it was his turn, which took a little extra effort. Since the box was so tall, he had to climb up some wooden crates that he had previously put into place, like a makeshift stairway.

Angelica could hear her father scrambling, his footfalls scrunching against the wood and the squealing of cardboard as he rubbed against the material. She thought for sure he would be discovered, but her ears heard nothing but silence for several seconds. Then a horrible smell slithered into her nostrils. It reminded her of a dead rat she had once seen on the road, being eaten away by insects. Two demons rattled down the steps into the basement, their footfalls heavy as they had nothing to fear.

Listening intently, Angelica could hear the monsters stomping around the room, knocking over furniture, and ripping through boxes. Suddenly, their steps grew in magnitude. Her compartment moved as one of the demons pushed at the large boxes next to her, and then she could hear it reaching inside, pulling out items, and throwing them to the floor. Then the creature shuffled to her box, repeating the action. She covered her mouth, her heavy breathing sounding like a thunderstorm, sweat glistening on her forehead.

Even though it was hard to understand, she heard one of the demons shout, “That’s taking too long, move out of the way!”

A strange noise entered Angelica’s ears. It almost sounded like a long whistle, or at least someone attempting to whistle. Over and over, the noise repeated itself several times, and then she heard it just above her. The box shuddered, and she knew the noise had been produced by something being pushed into her cardboard sanctuary.

It didn’t take her long to figure out what that something was, as a sharpened spear plunged through the cardboard. She jerked her head back, squeezing into her mother’s chest as the weapon barely missed her face. The long stick was removed, and then she heard one of the demons say, “There isn’t anything here. Let’s go.”

Angelica wiped the sweat from her brow as she heard the creatures shuffle off and leave the basement. A small sigh of relief escaped her shaking lips, and she thanked God for her family’s good fortune. Unfortunately, not everyone was as lucky as they. A few minutes later, the piercing screams of Mr. Mcgregor filled the room as the creatures dragged him away to one of their work camps. Luckily his wife Teresa and her son Jimmy were hiding in another basement and escaped detection.

Jimmy had been Angelica’s best friend for as long as she could remember. He was a year older than she and had red curly hair with matching freckles that sprinkled across his nose and cheeks. He was tall for his age and towered nearly an entire foot above her. Most of the people she knew, including herself, had a bedraggled appearance, wearing nothing more than tattered rags. But after the loss of his father, Jimmy’s appearance seemed even more out of sorts. The boy looked tired and worn, weighed down by sadness.

Jimmy never talked very much, and even less since the

day the demons took his father. Still, he had always been a great friend and listened to everything Angelica had to say. He was the only one who knew her secret. Even though her parents would be angry, she let Jimmy know that she prayed to God every night. He swore to her that he would never tell anyone, not even his mother.

That night while she was trying to find the stars, Jimmy quietly climbed up the roof and sat down beside her. He didn't say anything, which was typical of Jimmy. They just sat there in silence, staring into the sky, as they had many times in the past. She had hoped that he would start to come out of his shell, but obviously, she would have to be the one to break the silence.

"How have you been?" Angelica inquired as she looked up into Jimmy's face.

"I'm okay," Jimmy replied in an automated fashion.

"I'm worried about you. You're not the same anymore. I know you miss your dad, but you can't let that stop you from having some fun."

"Fun?" said Jimmy in a questioning and angry tone. "What can possibly be fun in this rotten world? Half of the time, we're starving. The other half, we're hiding from the demons."

"We can't give in to darkness. God will show us the way to the light," Angelica replied. "One day, I'm going to find those bright stars in the sky, and nothing will ever stop me from trying."

Jimmy jumped up to his feet and screamed, "You and your stupid stars! God isn't going to save us! He abandoned us a long time ago! You're just a stupid little girl, and I could care less what you think! You have your father! I'll never see my dad again!"

Without a backward glance, Jimmy ran down the side of the roof and quickly climbed down the ladder. Angelica watched him leave with tears in her eyes. She knew he was hurting, but he had never spoken that way to her before. Losing his dad had changed him, but Angelica couldn't blame him. If she lost her dad, she might react the same way. Her parents told her that God said to keep your heart open and forgive those who hurt you. She knew Jimmy couldn't mean the things he had said, so she would give him some time to calm down and talk to him again tomorrow.

Momentarily putting away her sorrow, the young girl wiped the tears from her face and peered out to the east. It wasn't completely dark yet, so she could still see path 45. One side of the road was almost completely devoid of any obstacles, but thousands of cars and trucks filled the far side from the northern to the southern horizon. To Angelica, they looked like an army of steel cockroaches blanketing a discarded belt, left to rot, twisted on their sides and back, waiting to be eaten, but too hard for anything or anyone to chew.

As far as the eye could see in either direction, long lines of concrete, steel, and rubble ran parallel to the path. Occasionally one building would vault proudly upward, untouched, flaunting its survival against the apocalypse. Hundreds of signposts both large and small littered the area. Some were torn entirely from the ground, while others still stood, contorted at strange angles. Dead trees lay scattered on the surface, rotting away, a constant reminder of how easily they were vanquished from their picturesque glory.

Turning completely around, Angelica continued her star search in a different direction. As she did this, she squinted, thinking she observed something moving across the desert. The young girl rubbed her eyes and blinked, putting her hand across her eyebrows like a visor, but whatever she thought she had seen was lost behind a small hill. Eyes glaring at the hill, an overwhelming feeling of doom wretched in her gut. Slowly dark figures started to emerge, one at a time from the far side of the prominence. They were still a long distance away, but she already knew what they were. Her feet were already moving as her heartbeat quickened, transmitting the signal to flee to her body.

She had to warn everyone. Demons were heading their way...

Abraham

Abraham continued his march up the steps, dragging his tired feet along each stair. Only ten more floors remained, but his thighs already burned in agony. After all these years, you would think his muscles would have built up some immunity to the pain. However, it seemed the older he got, the worst the pain became. He was only fifty years old, but on some days, he felt like he was seventy, and today was one of those days. He needed the Master's touch again, and only through his blessing could he remain young forever. This was the gift the Master had given him many years ago, but the power was only temporary.

As he reached the next landing, he thought back to those days, long ago, before the Master had saved him and showed him the path to glory. Ray jumped into his mind once again, the memory plaguing his thoughts as it had many times through the years. The cobwebs cleared, and he returned to his youth, taking the form of a twelve-year-old boy.

The bell rang, and he jetted out the door, quickly sprinting down the hallway to his brother's classroom. Abraham idolized his brother Ray as only a little brother can. Ray was fourteen and the best athlete in school. The boy's body radiated power, as every muscle was attached precisely to his above-average frame. His hair was jet black, tousled in the front, but neatly cut on the sides of his head. His face was broad, even making his cheeks look muscular, and his eyes were a large almond color. The girls chased after him like he was the only boy left in the world, but strangely he didn't seem interested in their advances. Sports was the only thing Ray cared about, and he was definitely made for it. He excelled in every sport he played and could already outrun the fastest varsity football players.

Actually, everyone in Abraham's family had been blessed with physical strength and speed. That is, except for him. Abraham somehow seemed to have missed out on inheriting that gene. Looking at the young boy was like looking at a Halloween skeleton. An entire state of research experts wouldn't be able to find muscles on his scrawny, little body.

However, a lack of physical ability seemed to be balanced out by brain capacity. Abe shined in every subject and was always the smartest kid in his class, but unfortunately, that brought him more negative attention than positive. Like bees flock to honey, the bullies flocked to his skinny stature, narrow face, and enormous spectacles. But this didn't last for long. Ray made sure of that.

Abraham had almost made it to Ray's classroom when Bobby Thorton shoved him into the lockers. Hitting the lockers with such great force that he lost his balance and nose-dived into the floor. The warm blood entered his mouth and dripped down his chin. He could already feel the numbing pain as his nose throbbed like a rock star's speaker turned to max. Keeping his eyes downward as they filled with tears, he could hear Bobby laughing hysterically along with several other kids. Bobby was one of those kids who lashed out at anyone more intelligent than he, and that was most of the seventh-grade class.

Lying there on the cold floor, Abe was too ashamed to look up. All of a sudden, the laughter ceased, and all that remained was utter silence. He started to raise his eyes, thinking that the principal must be standing above him, but instead, he raised his eyes and looked straight into his brother's. Those eyes burned hot red as Ray's face twitched and contorted. In a flash, Bobby was on the floor, straddled by his brother, as Ray relentlessly pounded him with his fists. Punch after punch rained down on poor Bobby, with all the strength Ray could muster. The bones cracked as the blood splattered and began to form puddles on the floor. All the while, Ray was screaming at the top of his lungs like a monster possessed. Abraham knew that Bobby Thorton would die that day if Ray wasn't stopped, but no one seemed to care. All the other kids just stood there mesmerized, either by fear or shock, in what they were witnessing.

Abraham shouted, "Ray, stop, you're going to kill him!"

But Ray was lost in blood lust and continued screaming and pounding away on poor Bobby's face. Bobby went limp, his arms dropping to the floor like wet noodles, but Ray continued pummeling him fist after fist, bone-cracking blow after bone-cracking blow.

"Someone stop him!" shouted Abraham.

No one moved.

Abraham crawled to his feet as quickly as possible in his injured state and ran to his brother. Grabbing Ray by the shoulders, he pulled with all his might, but it was futile. Ray was built like an ox, and in his enraged state, he seemed almost superhuman. He shook Abraham off with ease, spilling the young boy back to the floor. Abe watched as Ray lifted his fist, hovering it high in the air like a meteorite. He was sure this would be the final death blow to poor Bobby Thorton.

A blur crossed Abraham's vision as Principal Rivera tackled Ray to the ground. Two other teachers jumped in, and it took all their effort to restrain Ray in his crazed frame of mind. Locking his arms behind his back, they picked the teenager up and dragged him down the hallway toward the front office.

Nurse Brown was already attending to Bobby, and Abraham faintly remembered her calling for an ambulance. However, Bobby Thorton or his own throbbing nose was the least of Abe's concerns. He had to get to his brother. *Why did Ray act so crazy?* Now that he thought about it, Ray seemed to be very temperamental lately. But the way he behaved today was so out of the ordinary for his brother. *Something is seriously wrong with him.*

Still shaking, Abraham stumbled down the hallway, trying to catch up with Principal Rivera and his brother. *I must tell Mr. Rivera that Ray was only defending me, and he shouldn't be punished.* Abe was almost to the office when Mr. Williams, the science teacher, came out of the door and blocked his way.

"Abraham, where do you think you're going?" commanded Mr. Williams, as he grabbed the boy by the shoulders and turned him around.

Abe replied with despair in his voice, "I - I need to speak with Mr. Rivera. Ray shouldn't be punished. He was only protecting me!"

"Yes, we know. Father Rick has already been informed, and he's walking across from the church right now. He'll take care of everything. Clean that blood off your face and get to your next class before Father Rick sees you."

Abraham exhaled, the tension draining from his body and putting the young boy at ease. Father Rick was the leader of their parish and also the head football coach. He was a monster of a man, towering well over six feet, maybe closer to seven, and he tipped the scales at just under three-hundred pounds. His face was rough, even abrasive, lined with a thick, black mustache and bushy eyebrows, topped off with a short crop of grey hair. Everyone was afraid of Father Rick, including Mr. Rivera, but he was known to be a just man everyone admired, especially Ray. After all, he was a priest who spoke directly to God. Father Rick would know that Ray was innocent and would find out the truth to whatever was troubling his brother.

Ray and Abraham were both altar boys and helped Father Rick with mass every morning. Ray even had the privilege of staying late, after mass, to help Father Rick clean the church.

Abraham had always been jealous of this fact and prayed every night that Father Rick would choose him instead. He desperately wanted Father Rick to give him the attention that his brother was so lucky to receive. Surely Father Rick would take care of his favorite pupil Ray. With a smile from ear to ear, Abraham headed back to his classroom. All his earlier worries had melted away.

The third period breezed by, and the lunch bell rang. Abraham couldn't wait to talk to Ray and find out what Father Rick had to say. Sprinting as fast as he could, his little legs dashed to the cafeteria, nearly tripping on several occasions and being warned by more than one teacher to slow down. He grabbed his lunch and plopped his rear on the hard plastic seat in his usual spot near the windows. Abraham and Ray always sat together, and Abe kept looking over his shoulder toward the door in anticipation of his brother's return. However, the minutes ticked by, and Ray never came.

Abe engulfed his sandwich and apple, not even realizing he was eating, as his eyes remained glued to the big clock hanging against the far wall. Twenty minutes passed, and still no Ray. Abraham's mind began to race through dozens of possibilities. *Did they suspend him? Is he serving detention with Father Rick? Did they kick him off the football team?* Abraham drummed the table with his fingers, eyes darting back and forth from the clock to the door. Then he saw Mr. Rivera enter and head in his direction.

He waved the man over and asked, "Mr. Rivera, where's my brother?"

"Don't worry about him. Father Rick took him back to his house so he could receive his punishment."

Abraham began to chew on his lower lip as he pondered the dilemma that faced his brother. He didn't want to see Ray punished, but he knew there had to be some repercussions for what he had done to Bobby Thorton. Some of the other kids told him the ambulance took Bobby out on a stretcher, but apparently, he would live. Abraham thanked the Lord and hoped his injuries weren't too serious.

Lunch ended, and period after period ticked by through the afternoon. During each passing period, Abraham would hurry over to Ray's classes to see if he was there; but each time, he was disappointed. *Why hasn't he come back yet?* There was still one more class left before school let out, but Abe couldn't wait any longer. Curiosity gnawed at him, forcing him to take action.

While all the other kids were shuffling into their final class of the day, Abe stealthily snuck to the back door of the long hallway. Eyes like an eagle, he watched the teachers greet the students, ensuring they weren't looking in his direction. Quickly but with soft hands, he pushed the door open, stepped outside, and gently closed the door. Abe stood silent for a moment, pricking up his ears, expecting the sounds of approaching footfalls. But nothing happened. Father Rick's house was across the parking lot, next to the church. If he was quick, then maybe he could make it without anyone seeing him.

Heart pumping and knees lifting, the young boy started off, thinking he would hear Mr. Rivera yelling his name at any minute. His steps pounded the hard blacktop, frail legs and arms doing their comical best to exert the energy necessary. The church loomed ahead, its high belltower casting a shadow toward Father Rick's home.

It was hot that day, just like every day in Southern Texas. The sweat rolled down his neck and shoulders, leaking into his armpits, forming a puddle of uneasiness as steam rose from the dark floor in front of him, blurring his vision of the church.

Young Abe ducked behind a giant evergreen tree, panting like a dog in heat, wiping the sweat from his eyes. *I made it!* Arms shaking, he peered toward the school, sure to see Mr. Rivera heading his way, but no one was coming.

The church was lined with a row of evergreens, each one spiraling upward nearly twenty feet, arms expanded, like silent sentinels, ready to protect the church from harm. A small space remained between the trees and the church, so Abe scurried along the leeway until he was behind the building. Now it would be just a short hop over to the house, and he covered that in a few seconds without incident.

The house was simple, long, and narrow, only one story high. Red brick adorned the first four feet from the ground up, while the rest was covered by pearl-white siding. The yard was impeccably groomed; beautiful reddish, purple orchids lined the front and sides. Breathing deeply from his harrowing escape, the smell of fresh-cut grass bombarded Abraham's nostrils. It was still wet from the sprinklers, and stickily hitchhiked a ride on his shoes as he crossed the yard.

What do I do next? He hadn't really thought it through. Should he knock on the door and ask for his brother? This was sure to get him in trouble for skipping class, so instead, he decided to peek through the windows, but he couldn't see anyone. There was one window toward the back that he couldn't see through because the shades were closed. He could hear strange noises coming from it, so apparently, Father Rick must have forgotten to turn off the television.

Gingerly, Abe walked around to the front of the house and checked the doorknob, noticing it wasn't locked. *Should I peek my head inside*? He had to know where his brother was, regardless of what happened to him. Slowly, he opened the door, a slight creek moaning its displeasure, and then he stuck his head through the opening.

The living room was to the right, a long blue sofa was against the back wall, and an old rocking chair sat near the window facing the church. The kitchen was to the left, a white refrigerator surrounded by dark brown cabinets, stood against the farthest wall, with a small table and two chairs placed in the center of a grey tile floor.

"Father Rick are you here?" young Abe squeaked.

There was no answer, but he could hear the noises from the back room, even louder now that the front door was open. With ninja-like steps, he entered the house and started creeping down the hallway toward the room, passing an open bathroom to his right. A magazine lay on the floor next to the toilet; naked people in different positions stared at him from the pages. Covering his eyes, he quickly moved on, not knowing what to make of the unusual pictures. He could still hear the muffled sounds coming from the last door but couldn't quite make out what they were. Each step brought him closer to the door and closer to translating the gargled sounds.

Finally, he reached the door and was able to make out what was being said. "Do you like your punishment, Ray?" he heard Father Rick ask.

"Yes, Sir!" Ray shouted.

Then Abraham heard a loud smacking sound, and Ray screamed in agony. He could hear Ray moaning in pain but didn't know what to do. He knew Ray had to be punished, but the sounds he was making really sounded painful. Father Rick needed to hear his side of the story.

Slowly, he opened the door and peeked inside. What he saw would be a memory that, unfortunately, would stay firmly written in his mind for the rest of his life. He should have looked away, but he couldn't. Unknowingly in a trance-like state, he entered the room and closed the door behind him. It seemed like he was walking through a dream and couldn't control his actions. Father Rick's naked back was to him. Without even realizing he had done it, Abraham picked up a heavy iron lamp from the dresser.

With all the force his skinny arms could muster, he drove the lamp into Father Rick's back, driving him to his knees. Father Rick turned, his naked body covered in perspiration and a look of puzzlement in his eyes. Abraham pulled the lamp back again and drove it forward into Father Rick's skull with all his might.

The priest fell to the floor, but that wasn't the end of it. The veins pulsed on his forehead as Abraham swung again, over and over. He couldn't stop himself.

As the blood flew up onto his face, the only thing Abe could think was that he was just like his big brother. He had now switched roles and became the monster that was beating up Bobby Thorton. Robot-like, Abe couldn't remember how many times he hit Father Rick, but when he was finished nothing remained but mush. Looking down, all he could see were bits of the Father's brain strewn across the floor.

Feeling the eyes upon him, he turned and saw Ray looking at him with bulging eyes and a quivering lip. How long his brother had been staring at him, he couldn't fathom, but it didn't matter. As Abe looked at him, all he could think was, *how could you let this happen?* His brother stood there naked, his wiener hanging loose like a little worm. His face was a mask of stupidity, dull eyes staring back at him with no answer. *You're not the hero I admired. You look weak. You're pitiful.* He was disgusted by the boy standing in front of him. Abraham's arms felt like they weighed a thousand pounds, but they still had enough strength for one more swing. With every ounce he could call upon, he pulled back and drove the lamp forward into his brother's head. Ray fell like a cut tree, landing next to Father Rick, blood streaming out of his skull.

That was the day long ago that Abraham came to believe that God didn't exist, and he started his new journey of enlightenment. His thoughts returned to the present as he took the last step and reached the door to the penthouse. Showing great concern for his appearance, Abraham tucked in his shirt and brushed back his hair. Nervously but also with a tinge of excitement, he opened the door and prepared to see his Master.

The Dead Forest

Our trio continued down the worn path numbered 45. Sometimes the way was lost to us as it was covered in thick dirt, but eventually, if we searched hard enough, we would find the road once again. Sporadically, we would see signs that told us how many more miles to the next village, but sometimes these villages didn't exist. Maybe they did long ago, but the Last War had wiped them from the map, never to return. We had recently passed a partially destroyed sign, with only some of the letters remaining visible. It read – Hunt vill, so I surmised that the name must have been Hunter Village. I hoped this was true because our supplies were running low, and we could definitely do with some fresh meat.

We continued traveling for several more miles alone in our own thoughts. Then the scenery slowly began to change, and in the distance, something began to form on the horizon, but I couldn't make it out at first.

"What is that?" I asked Bill, who was riding to my left.

"I'm not sure. It looks like a giant wall from east to west."

"It could be mountains."

"No way, dumb-ass. Mountains aren't all the same height. Look, as far as you can see, they're consistent."

Bill was right. They appeared to be the same height. We continued plodding forward until there was a long dip in the path, causing us to lose sight of the strange phenomenon. After a few minutes, we came back up the hill, and I looked through narrowed eyes to solve the mystery.

"They're trees!" I exclaimed.

"Your right," Bill responded. "Thousands of them."

Bill sorely underestimated the number. For as far as the eye could see, there was a wall of dead trees. There were probably millions of them. We had never seen so many trees in our travels, and I remembered the old word – forest. This brought me high in my saddle, and a smile crossed my face from one ear to the other. Forests meant game!

"There could be deer in there!" I shouted in exuberance.

"My stomach is growling," replied Bill. "I'm so hungry I would prefer eating deer to having sex!"

Bill's response caused a chuckle to escape my lips, but I couldn't argue his logic, for it had been a long time since we had eaten deer. As a matter of fact, it may have been a few years. Lately, the only thing we had eaten was bugs, snakes, and lizards. It had even been quite a while since we had eaten a dog. I don't know if I can believe the old stories, but it's been said that before the Last War, every person owned a dog or cat. What's truly amusing is the elders say people didn't eat them. What purpose could there possibly be to have a cat or dog if you're not going to eat it? Sometimes I think the elders were just messing with us.

Licking our lips in anticipation, we continued moving forward, and in a few minutes, we entered the path between the woods. The dead trees reached up from the barren soil, most of their dark trunks pointing at least five stories up toward the heavens, like an army of rusted swords, hoping that God would fall upon them. As we passed, I touched one and felt the bark crumble to dust in my hand. How so many of them remained standing was a mystery for the ages.

Most of the branches were gone, but the few that remained produced an eerie feeling, interlocking with their partners to create a barrier of claustrophobia. We couldn't discern any leaves on any of them, but we could make out weeds growing in patches on the ground, adamantly trying to return life to the grim forest of death, and wherever there were weeds, there was a chance that something would want to eat them.

Our dark friend guided his horse from the main path and entered the forest. Bill and I followed him closely, keeping as quiet as possible. As we moved, I felt the breeze scramble into my nostrils, and I breathed deeply, taking in the scent of the forest. The smell of life would have been a scintillating reward, but instead, I only absorbed musty decay and dirt.

Occasionally, our dark companion dismounted, picking at the dirt, rummaging through the weeds, and searching the area for tracks. This was a painstakingly slow process but necessary all the same. Our search went on for hours, but finally, we were rewarded. Our brooding friend pointed at the tracks profoundly dug into the dirt ahead, and we could clearly tell they were the hoof marks of a deer. Bill and I looked at each other and started bouncing in our saddles like a child discovering a new toy. Smiling, I gave him a thumbs-up sign while he made an obscene gesture, turning his hands into a female body part, and hungrily licking the shape.

We dismounted, tethered our horses to the trees, and decided to go the rest of the way by foot. Our dark friend took the lead, following the tracks like a whisper in the wind. Occasionally, he would stop, eyes wide open, searching for the prey. Bill and I constantly scanned the area from side to side. We weren't only looking for game but making sure nothing was hunting us. After all, demons also get hungry.

Diligently, we wound our way through the tree trunks, following the tracks for nearly thirty minutes. It was a slow and tedious process, but finally, we were compensated for our patience. Our dark leader lifted his hand, signaling us to stop. We could barely make out a rustle of weeds and branches toward the South. It was probably one hundred yards away, but something had definitely moved from one tree bole to the next. The big guy put a finger to his lips and continued in the same direction, which would circle him around to the right of our prey. Bill and I decided to move in from the left.

After a few minutes, we could no longer see our leader, but regardless, Bill and I continued to creep closer, feet squishing in the soft mud as we used the trees for cover. The terrain sloped down slightly at this point, causing us to briefly lose sight of our quarry. Laying on our bellies, we crawled a few more feet, and that's when we heard the animal eating. But something didn't seem right. It didn't sound like a deer eating weeds or dead grass, and then the wind shifted, and the rank odor filled our senses. The stench was unusual. I could clearly smell blood, but it seemed to be mixed with something else.

Once, about a year ago, we had found a bottle of rotten maple syrup in an abandoned house. This is the only thing I could compare the stench to, as the wind dragged the strange smell toward us. We crawled up the slight incline on our stomachs, little by little until the deer finally came into view.

My eyes nearly exploded from their sockets as our prey was revealed. The deer wasn't the one eating; instead, it was being eaten by the most gigantic wild boar we had ever seen. The beast had to stand nearly six feet tall at the shoulder, and I estimate it weighed well over one thousand pounds. Its color camouflaged perfectly with the forest, brown like the soil, and a ring of black fur surrounded its neck. Enormous sharp tusks jetted out from the sides of its snout. These wicked daggers dived back and forth into the belly of the deer, shredding it open with ease. The animal's entire face was soaked in blood, dripping from its jowls, as it cut its way in and devoured its meal.

We did not want to mess with this thing, regardless of how hungry we were. Looking at Bill, I signaled for him to retreat, and we were just about to move when we heard noises coming from behind us. Our jaws dropped to the floor when we turned and saw what was making the commotion. The monster we had watched wasn't alone. It traveled in a pack, and they had found us. There had to be at least ten of them, and they were all just as big or bigger than the first monstrosity we had seen. We thought the first boar we had tracked was a freak of nature, but one in the group was near twice its size.

Both of us tried to remain as still as possible, hoping that the creatures would ignore us. They were too close, so outrunning them was not an option. The trees closest to us provided no protection, as I realized that none of them had branches low enough to climb. For a brief second, I thought, what could the animals be thinking? Then one of the monster's eyes met mine, and it charged. The muscles expanded underneath its skin in an almost rhythmic pattern as it flew towards me, tusks lowered, ready to tear me to pieces.

Bill said, "What a great way to die, --- eaten by a pig."

Betrayal

Angelica stumbled and tripped, her hands scraping against the worn shingles and exposed plywood. In an instant, she was up again, moving as rapidly as she could down the roof without falling. Swinging herself quickly onto the ladder, the small girl started the twenty-foot descent. Halfway down, she missed one of the rungs and slipped. Luckily her hands slowed her down, flailing at each rung as she fell to the ground. Unfortunately, her chin also hit some of the steps, and she smacked her teeth together. The coppery taste of blood formed on her tongue, and she was afraid she had chipped her teeth, but she didn't have time to dwell on that now. She had to warn her parents and the rest of the community.

The building she watched the stars from was closest to the old road but farthest from all the inhabited homes on the other side of the village. Her parents had warned her not to go that far away, but it was the tallest building standing in the area, and she thought that maybe she would have a better chance at seeing the stars from that elevation. Her wishful thinking had cost her and now meant she would have to run almost a mile to get to her parents.

All these thoughts rushed through her head as she covered the distance. Praying to God to give her strength, she pumped her little legs as fast as she could, knees rocketing toward the sky and arms digging at the air. Each step caused little puffs of dust to explode upward behind her, like mini volcanoes erupting into the atmosphere.

With the muscles in her legs screaming to be reprieved, she passed the half-way mark. The young girl had never pushed herself so hard, and she was afraid she wouldn't make it, but she couldn't give up hope. *I'll never give up!* Angelica would sacrifice all the pain in the world if it saved her parents. God's son had offered his life for the love of the world. She could sacrifice hers for the life of her family.

Renewed determination helped the young girl dig in her heels, propelling her even faster. That's when she saw her dad crossing the street. She opened her mouth and tried to scream, but she was breathing so hard that the words became stuck in her throat. Angelica's dad turned his head, his eyes doubling in size as he looked in her direction. However, his eyes didn't remain focused on her for long. She could tell he was looking behind her. The man bolted her way like a track star, at the same time frantically yelling for Angelica's mom.

Her dad covered the distance quickly, sweeping her up and crushing her into his arms. There was no time to ask questions as he spun around and took off as fast as possible. Face resting on his shoulder, and her legs clamped around his waist, she could now see behind her. The demons were close. Close enough to see her and her dad. *They know we're here. Even if we hide, they'll keep looking until they find us.*

Rounding the corner into a side street caused her to lose sight of the monsters. Her father jumped over a broken signpost, almost tripping, his right leg buckling for a moment, but he caught his balance and continued on his way.

By this time, the young girl's mother had heard her husband's calls and was running toward them. As they came together, her dad handed Angelica to her mom and screamed, "Hide her. They're almost here!"

She watched her father warn the others as her mother ducked into the house, bringing her down the stairs into the basement. The room was dark except for some light seeping through a few narrow cracks in the ceiling. Old furniture was piled like it usually was, in no particular order across the entire left wall. Jimmy and his mom were already there, hiding behind the large boxes stacked against the right wall.

Wanting to comfort her friend, Angelica ran to Jimmy to hug him, but he turned from her and hugged his mother instead. *He's still mad at me, and I don't blame him. He's probably thinking about the last time the demons came and took his dad. I'm sure he's worried that this time they'll take his mom.*

A tear rolled down her cheek as she thought about Jimmy, but right now, her main concern was her own father. The demons had seen him, so hiding wasn't an option. He was still young enough to work in the Hus-town slave camps so they wouldn't kill him. Her stomach twisted as she realized she would never see him again.

A few minutes passed, and then she heard a demon shout in its gargled speech, "Stop right there, and tell the others to come out!"

"There aren't any others. I'm alone," her father responded.

Angelica heard the demon stomp across the ceiling, dust falling through the cracks. Then a large clapping noise reached her ears, followed by a moan from her father.

"I saw the little girl!" the demon screamed. "Tell them to come out, or I'll hit you again!"

Angelica's dad wouldn't say a word. The young girl buried her face in her mother's stomach and covered her ears as she heard the beasts beating her father. After a few minutes, one of the demons commanded the others in its group to search the houses. Angelica, Jimmy, and their moms climbed into the large boxes, and Angelica's mother slipped in the false tops.

From the safety of her box, Angelica could hear the screams of other people in her community as the demons dragged them outside into the street. Just when she thought they might have been lucky, she heard the creaking of the stairs as someone came down into the basement. Breathing heavily, her heart pounded so hard she was afraid it would burst through her chest. She had to calm herself, or the creatures might hear her. Covering her mouth, her mother gently ran her fingers through the young girl's hair. Angelica's heartbeat began to slow, and after a few moments, her breath returned to normal.

Angelica could hear something shuffling around the room. Wood splintered as furniture was flipped over and boxes crumbled as they were kicked across the room. The noises seemed to be coming from the opposite side of the basement. Demons weren't very bright, so Angelica hoped they would be able to trick them once again. Then complete silence filled the room, and she thought the creatures were finished, but her hopes were soon dashed as loud footsteps, and heavy breathing headed their way.

A strong thud rocked her shoulder as the demon kicked the box, knocking it over and causing all the contents to spill out. The monster must have seen that the bottom of the box wasn't deep enough and yanked it out, revealing Angelica and her mother. The creature screamed and continued kicking all the boxes in a frenzy, tearing them open until it also discovered Jimmy and his mom. It reached down, wrapping its gruesome fingers around Jimmy and Angelica's hair, yanking violently, and started to drag them toward the stairs. The two moms tried grabbing the brute by the shoulders, but with a swing of its fist, he knocked them both to the floor.

"Follow me, or I'll slit their throats!"

Reluctantly, the children's moms dragged their feet up the stairs with downcast heads while the creature continued pulling the kids by the hair. The monster dragged them outside and dumped them in line with the rest of the humans.

The leader of the demon pack strutted up and down the line with arms crossed, snarling as he glared at the people they had captured. The creature was a huge brute, towering probably six and a half feet, and even though it was skinny, the demon probably still weighed close to two-hundred pounds. It had a deep scar running across its cheek, dripping with a pinkish puss. The puss would splatter on its bare chest, seeping into hundreds of open sores, intermingling with more puss, like some grotesque map, covered by islands made of mucous. The monster's eyes were completely white like all the other demons, and its skin looked even rougher and more shriveled than most. Most people would feel disgusted when they looked at a demon. --- Angelica could only feel pity.

The beast stopped, directly in front of the brown-haired girl, glanced down, and said, "So this is the one that saw us. She runs pretty fast for one so little."

The creature continued its march but raised its voice and said, "We are taking all the men and five women. The other women can stay here with the children."

Angelica looked at her parents and started to cry. She started praying to God in her mind, begging him to stop them from taking her mother. *Please, Lord, don't let me lose both of my parents.* The demon leader started moving down the line, squeezing arms and shoulders, checking how strong the humans were as if he were inspecting cattle. First, he picked Mrs. Hickon, then Mrs. Hernandez, third was Mrs. Wood, and fourth Mrs. Sanchez. The creature only needed one more, and Angelica's mother was next in line. Angelica closed her eyes and continued praying harder, and then the demon brushed past them and stopped in front of Jimmy's mom.

Opening her eyes, she heard the demon leader say, "And this one."

Her eyes shot to Jimmy, and he returned the look, but the stare he gave wasn't a look of friendship. The boy's lips quivered, his eyebrows furrowed, and his nose scrunched into a prune.

"No, you can't take her!" Jimmy blurted.

The lead demon abruptly turned with raised eyebrows and pulled back its hand to strike little Jimmy. Before the blow could land, Jimmy quickly responded, "If you don't take her, then I will tell you which of them still prays to God!" This stopped the demon's downward swing, and instead, a wicked smile crept across its dark face.

Angelica whispered *No* as she dug her fingers into her thighs like the screeching of a chalkboard. Jimmy slowly pointed his finger directly at her and said, "Her and her parents pray to the false God every night!"

"He lies!" Angelica's parents screamed in unison. "We don't even know what God is!"

The demon leader screamed, "Silence!" and walked over to Angelica. The creature looked down at her and said, "Is this true, little one? Do you pray to the false God?"

Angelica looked at him without a hint of fear in her eyes and replied, "He isn't false. He is the one true God."

All at once, the demons started to scream in agony. It was almost like their skin was on fire, so great was the pain of Angelica's words. They grabbed her with steel fingers and started dragging her toward the old fountain in the center of the village. Angelica's parents tried to stop them, but they were beaten back. They rushed in for another attempt and were able to grab hold of her, but an onslaught of strikes from the demon's clubs knocked them nearly senseless to the ground.

The creatures reached the fountain and stretched Angelica across it, securing her arms and legs with a rope. Then they started chanting, praising Satan's name in their gargled, unholy speech. They circled the fountain, raising their frantic screams louder and louder, gesturing obscenely, tearing what little clothes they had from their twisted bodies, working themselves into a frenzy.

Then a loud voice boomed out, halting the demons where

they stood, as Angelica's parents screamed, "We taught her how to pray! She is innocent and doesn't understand! Take our lives instead!"

It was only a brief second that Angelica looked at her parents before the demons were upon them. Unable to turn her head away from the horror, she watched as they tore her parents apart. The demons yanked and pulled, bones snapping, flesh ripping, removing her parents' limbs from their bodies. They dug their fingers into her mothers' stomach, sharp nails cutting skin, blood gushing, boring deeper, finding and pulling out her intestines. Finally, Angelica's eyes remained zombie-like when they hacked her father's head off with a machete and tossed it from one demon to the next like some grisly toy.

When they were done, they returned to her and once again started their evil ritual. They continued chanting faster and faster. The demon leader pulled out his knife, and she smiled. *Maybe Jimmy is right. -- This is a rotten world. -- Maybe God has forgotten us, and death is the only savior.* The demon raised the knife high and started the blade's descent toward her heart.

Abraham And The Master

Abraham opened the door to the presidential suite. It had been an exhausting climb to the seventy-fifth floor. The JP Morgan Chase Tower was the tallest building in Houston, standing over one-thousand feet high. Actually, it had been the tallest building in Texas, even before the Last War. Almost all the buildings in Houston were destroyed during the nuclear blast, but somehow this building stood unscathed.

The Master told Abraham that he had saved the building for himself. Regardless, electricity didn't exist anymore, so the elevators didn't work, causing Abraham to make the long climb whenever he was called. But he didn't mind because he knew the Master was testing his Faith, and passing the test would lead to the reward he desired – immortality.

Abe crossed the long hallway into the lavish apartment. The most expensive and pretentious furniture was placed impeccably across the room. A gigantic golden chandelier hung from the ceiling, directly over a massive dining room table that could easily seat twenty people. Antique paintings from Da Vinci and Donatello hung on every wall, and the original statue of David stood proudly in the far corner, in all its splendor.

The Master was waiting for him near the windows; his back turned as he peered out across the city. The man was dressed as usual, in an expensive tailored black suit, and Abraham could see a magnificent Rolex watch, covered in diamonds, dangling from his right wrist. Abraham admired how dignified and powerful he looked, even with his back turned toward him.

Spinning around like a cat, the Master smiled at Abraham, and once again, Abe was left speechless. He thought to himself, *the Master must be the most handsome man I've ever seen.* His chin seemed to be chiseled from granite, set perfectly below his radiant white teeth. The man's skin was as perfect as a young child, blemishes impossible to discover, and his long hair a shade of honey blond that seemed to glow like the brightest fire. Finally, those incredible dark blue eyes that seemed to pierce right through him. The Master took a step forward and ferociously hugged Abraham.

"It is good to see you, Abe. You look a little tired."

"It is nothing, my Lord. Just a little pain in my knees." Abraham replied, still entranced by the Masters' beauty.

"That's something I can take care of, but do you deserve it?"

Flabbergasted, Abraham replied, "Master, you know I would do anything for you. You have given me so much!"

Without any further delay, the Master asked, "What word of this warrior from the North?"

"He was last seen near Huntsville, before the great forest."

"Did you send word that he should not be detained?"

"Yes, my Lord, but I do not understand. Why not have him killed?"

The Master chuckled. "He has a purpose to serve that will satisfy me greatly. That is all you need to know, Abraham, and if you want me to bless you with my touch, then make sure he comes to me unmolested."

"Yes, my Lord," Abraham replied with a bow and a smile on his face.

The Master signaled for Abraham to leave, and even though his knees hurt, he turned with renewed vigor in his step. Leaving the apartment, he started the long descent down the stairs. As he traveled, he kept praising the Master and imagined his touch once again.

Thinking back, he remembered when he first met the Master and felt that powerful touch. It was only moments after he ended his brother's miserable existence. Looking down at Father Rick and Ray's dead bodies, his body shook as a cold chill ran down his spine. An overwhelming feeling that someone was watching him entered his mind. Spinning around, Abe's eyes nearly popped from his skull as he observed the most beautiful man he had ever seen. The man stood only a few steps away with arms wide open in a gesture of peace and benevolence.

Then the man opened his mouth and spoke. To Abraham, his voice sounded like every desire he had ever wanted. He pictured gorgeous women lusting after him and the most delicious ice cream and candy piled to the ceiling, waiting for him to devour. Images of himself driving the most expensive sports cars and owning mansions with servants flashed across his vision. Finally, he saw a life without pain or worry.

The man said, "The God you have worshipped has brought you nothing but pain. He is a lie. It was him that allowed Father Rick to rape your brother. And he is the one that denied your brother the strength to stop him. Why would you follow him?"

The words cut deep into Abraham's heart. He thought about all the days he attended mass and remembered the countless times Ray and he had helped Father Rick. How many times had he prayed to God? The number must have been in the thousands. All of this he had given to God, and what had God given to him? Nothing but sorrow! Nothing but ridicule! Nothing but pain!

The man spoke again with his magical tongue. "Deny him and follow me. I will make all your desires come true."

Staring at those amazing eyes, Abraham's body went limp, mouth hanging open, spit dripping from his lower lip. The beautiful man's arms looked so warm and comforting. They invited him in like a soft blanket wraps a baby. Abraham looked at the bodies lying on the floor, soaked in blood, and then at his own hands, the instruments of their deaths. The pain and fear inside his gut begged for relief. The desires this incredible man had shown him were vividly repeated in his thoughts, teasing him to succumb to their promises of happiness.

Abraham sucked in a deep breath, kneeled, and said with utter clearness in his voice, "I deny the false God and all he stands for. I beg you to be my Lord and Master."

The Master stepped forward and enveloped him, pulling his mind and body into another consciousness. Abraham felt a surging flood through his body. It pushed the pain and doubt away, replacing it with an ecstasy and confidence he had never known. No longer was he the weak little boy that was bullied for being too smart. Instead, he would be a king who would dominate, control, and watch others suffer.

As he approached the bottom of the tower, his reminiscing ended, and he came back to reality. Abraham realized how badly he needed to please his Master, and he wouldn't risk disappointing him. *I will personally find this warrior and bring him back to pay homage to my Master.* Leaving the building, he found his horse tethered where he had left it, mounted the beast, and headed north.

The Sacrifice

The pack charged toward us, hooves smashing through the undergrowth. Bill and I had already strung our bows when we crawled up the incline to observe the first beast. Pulling our arrows back with shaking hands, we fired in unison. For a brief instant, I thought we had taken two of the monsters down. They both tumbled, legs snapping, snouts crashing into the dirt, but then I realized both of our shots had missed wide, landing harmlessly in the weeds and broken branches. Then a blur moved past us, and our dark leader was already stringing his third arrow. He released the weapon with a resounding twang, the missile moving so fast that it seemed to disappear for a moment and then reappear, lodging in the brain of another beast.

Then he was in among them, both swords drawn, painting a picture of only one color, --- red. Bill and I could only stand there, jaws dropping, eyes bulging, as his swords slashed in and out, blood splattering everywhere. Every time a beast would charge in to gore him, he would jump up, push off the monster's back, and land behind him. One time it almost appeared that he was floating as he ran across the backs of several of the creatures. All the while, his swords were twirling so fast that Bill and I couldn't comprehend which of the boars he was striking. However, we could see many of the beasts slowing down. Some of them began to stumble on spaghetti legs, and one by one, they began to drop, blood seeping from lethal wounds.

Only one of the creatures remained, the giant leader of

the pack. The monster was so covered in blood that it was hard to find a spot that wasn't dark scarlet. The beast pawed at the ground, roots, and dirt flying in the air. It exploded forward, tusks lowered, saliva dripping from its mouth. For a moment, I thought my dark companion would not be able to escape. But once again, I doubted his supernatural abilities, only to be proven wrong. Spinning like a tornado, he sidestepped with blazing footwork in the final instant, swung both of his swords downward, and decapitated the beast, head toppling and rolling across the ground.

"Yassss!" shouted Bill with glee. "I guess I know what we're going to be eating for a while."

"Boar burgers sound good to me," I replied.

Our dark friend was already cutting up the meat as Bill and I approached.

"Is there anything you do that shouldn't surprise us?" I asked.

He just continued cutting as if we weren't even there.

"Hey, pin-head, don't even bother. He's too good to talk to us," said Bill.

Mouths dripping with anticipation, we helped him cut up the carcasses and gathered branches to build a fire. We had a large bag of salt in our backpack, but there was still no way we could possibly save that much meat. The rest would have to be left for whatever other predators roamed this forest.

As we were cutting the meat, I asked Bill, "How does he do it?"

"Do what, pin-head?"

"Overcome every obstacle thrown at him. He went through those boars with as much effort as it takes me to tie my shoes."

"He's not like us," replied Bill.

"No shit."

"Did you just swear?" Bill replied with a grin on his face. "You're becoming more like me every day."

"The day that happens, please kill me," I chuckled.

"What I meant, dummy, is I finally figured out what he is."

"What's that?" I asked with some actual hope of discovering the mystery.

"He's freaking Superman!" Bill flamboyantly said as he stuck his arms out and pretended to fly.

Hysterically, we burst out laughing and didn't stop until my cheeks hurt. It felt good to laugh. I hadn't laughed that hard in a long time, and I had almost forgotten how it felt. Finally, I stopped, breathing so heavy that if someone saw me, they would think I just finished running a marathon. Looking at our dark friend, I prayed our laughter would have brought even a tiny glimmer of a smile, but nothing happened, as his stoic face remained unmoving. *Will you ever show emotion? What will it take to break through the barrier that surrounds you? You need to move on with your life.*

I admired my dark friend like a big brother, but I also pitied him. After all these years, I had learned to love him, but I also came to hate his gloom. If I could ask God for one thing, it would be that before I died, I would see him smile.

Our group camped there that night under the trees, filling our bellies with roasted boar meat. We woke early the following day, stuffed our faces once again, and began retracing our steps back to path 45. The trip through the woods was uneventful, and we didn't catch a glimpse of any more animals on our way. Not that it would have mattered. Our packs were so full of meat that it wouldn't make any sense to hunt for anything else.

It took us a few hours, but we eventually found the path and headed toward Hus-town again. After about three hours, we exited the great forest, and from here, the land became flat with only sparse dead trees marking the landscape. We passed through the remains of a few small villages but didn't see any signs of human or demon life.

It was late afternoon when we decided to make a brief stop to eat and feed the horses. A sign along the road said Conroe was ten miles ahead, and at our current pace we would reach the village shortly after nightfall. Bill and I hoped our leader would stop there to rest, but you never knew what to expect from him.

"You think there are any women in Conroe?" Bill said. "I'm horny as a rabbit."

"Keep it in your pants," I responded. "I would be happy if I could just find a nice bed to lay on."

"That sounds good, but I would prefer to make a sandwich."

"A sandwich?" I asked curiously

"Yeah, a soft bed and me, with a woman in between."

Laughing at Bill's joke, I noticed the big guy was already mounting his horse, so Bill and I quickly finished eating, hopped on our horses, and resumed our journey south. Time clicked by without much discussion until we started seeing the remnants of Conroe on the horizon. As we approached, one structure stood out, looming at least two stories high. The rest of the buildings seemed to be only one level or nothing more than piles of rubble.

The closer we drew to the village, the more we could tell something was wrong. The sounds of gargled singing entered our ears, --- or could it be screaming in unison. At this point the big guy dug his spurs into his horse, driving the animal forward. Bill and I also launched our steeds into action, realizing the noise could only mean one thing. A human sacrifice was about to occur. From our previous encounters with demons, we knew if the chanting stopped, then it would be too late. Almost a mile away, we weren't sure if we could make it in time.

Pushing the horses as hard as possible, their hooves rattled along the blacktop like a ticking clock on steroids. Moving at this speed could be highly dangerous. The paths had deteriorated through the years, and there were many holes and cracks that could easily break a horse's ankle if it took a misstep. Nevertheless, this didn't slow our dark companion. He relentlessly moved forward, leaving caution to the wind.

Then the satanic chanting stopped, and the sound of a human voice yelling traveled to our eardrums. At first, we thought we were too late. Fearing that the sacrifice had already happened, we slowed our pace to prevent injuring the horses. We would still have time for revenge but losing the horses didn't make any sense now.

Suddenly the chanting started again, and we realized our mistake. The sacrifice wasn't over. --- Something had delayed it. Once again, we spurred our horses to top speed. We shouldn't have slowed down.

An intersection appeared ahead, and the sounds of demonic worship were much closer than before. Making the turn, horses furiously pounding dust in every direction, we saw a horde of the creatures moving in a circle about one hundred yards away. The monsters were blocking our view, but from experience, we could assume a human must be inside their beastly ring.

One of the demons was in the group's center, nearly a foot taller than the rest. The monstrosity raised a blade above its head, the metal giving off a reflective glimmer.

Our leader had already notched his bow when he entered the intersection. The best archers could accurately hit a target on a straight flight at fifty yards maximum, but we were at least eighty yards away. It would be an impossible shot. It won't get there on time, but he must try. Veins bulging in his forearm, left hand kneading into the grip of the bow, he pulled the string back to his cheek and released the arrow.

The Old Man

There weren't any buildings remaining near the Master's Tower. As a matter of fact, there wasn't anything at all. Everything had been vaporized from the nuclear blast leaving a vast crater for nearly half a mile in every direction. Either due to the scarcity of any livable buildings or fear of radioactivity, none of the demons ventured into this area. Abraham would need help to fulfill his mission, but he would have to begin his recruitment a little farther away.

Riding his horse through the desolate area, he realized he would need a much larger host than had previously encountered the warrior the Master sought. If the stories weren't exaggerations, then this mans' prowess with martial skill was unmatched. *I need a small army. Overkill is better than returning empty-handed to the Master.*

For a long time, Abe had been working on a plan that would significantly improve their odds, making them an invincible force. Currently, the demons only used whatever weapons they could find. This mainly consisted of clubs, knives, and occasionally, they came across a sword. However, most of the beasts didn't even have any weapons and simply used their hands. Abraham's plan was to create an armory and forge their own weapons.

It was pure luck that brought this idea to his mind. A year ago, he was out raiding towns with a host of demons when they came across a formidable foe. When his scouts didn't return, Abe rode his steed into the town, passing mutilated demon bodies, heads and limbs cleanly removed like they were slabs of beef at a meat market.

As he moved closer, he could hear soft steps scrunching the stones beneath them, weapons whisking through the air, and the gargled screams of demons. Abraham rounded the corner of a building, his eyes opening to the narrow alleyway before him, and as he did, he observed an old man slaughtering his demons with a sword.

The man was completely bald, dressed in loose-fitting orange robes. Deep wrinkles crossed his forehead and lined his cheeks, creating a pyramid from his nose to his mouth. His eyes were a piercing, chocolate brown that gave the impression of someone who commanded respect, but also fear from his enemies.

At closer inspection, the white eyebrows and heavy folds of wrinkles told the story of a man close to eighty years old, but time had somehow forgotten to rob him of his youth. He could still move fluidly, with both grace and power, displaying the speed of someone half his age. But after watching him for several minutes, Abraham ascertained his true advantage was his weapon. It was a Chinese straight sword, edged on both sides and pointed at the tip.

Abraham had seen swords like this in old Kung Fu movies before the Last War and had even held a few in his hand since then. However, this sword was nothing like those. If he didn't know better, he would think it was magical. The old man sliced through arms, knives, and clubs like they were butter.

One of the demons backed toward the corner of a building, sliding on the loose gravel as he made futile attempts to block the old man's attacks with his club. Each time the sword struck, pieces of the weapon fell off like the old man was a chef cutting through an onion. Then the old man lunged forward, sword swing horizontally, ready to remove the demon's head. The only thing that saved the creature was the loose gravel. As the demon stepped back, his foot slipped, causing his knee to buckle and dropping his head just enough to avoid the weapon. The sword continued its momentum and effortlessly sliced through the concrete wall behind the demon.

Abraham sucked in a deep breath through his mouth as his eyes swelled. *I need to know where that weapon came from.*

"Take him alive!" Abe commanded. "If you kill him, then the Master will punish you!"

Hearing their leader's words, the demons backed off to regroup. There were still seven of them remaining from the original group, and they were joined by another ten from Abraham's reinforcements. The demons huddled together to make a new plan as the old man sat down, crossed his legs, and began meditating.

The demons dispersed from their meeting, fanning out, creating a circle around the old man. The man sprung to his feet as one of the demons raised its arm. The creature dropped the arm, and all at once, the entire crew rushed in at full speed. When they came into range, the old man kept his sword facing outward at arm's length with the blade at waist level. Twisting his body, the sword moved in a circular motion, the blade slicing through bone and flesh, taking out several monsters. Unfortunately, their sheer numbers pushed the falling dead onto the old man and knocked him to the ground. He tried to get up, but the overwhelming weight of the creatures held him down until they finally disarmed him.

"Bring me that sword!" Abraham shouted at the demons as they restrained the old man.

Mounted on top of his horse, Abraham reached down as one of the demons handed him the sword. Abe grasped the handle, feeling the weight of the weapon. *It doesn't feel any different from any other sword that I've touched.*

Curiosity piqued, he maneuvered his horse next to an old stop sign. The sign was missing most of the octagon but still had the steel pole planted firmly in the concrete. Moving his arm as if he were treading water, he let the sword glide toward the pole. Incredibly, he felt no resistance as the weapon sliced through the object, toppling the upper section of the sign.

"This sword is amazing!" Abraham exclaimed with a broad grin as he trotted his horse over to stop in front of the old man. "Where did you get it?"

"I made it," the old man replied.

"Who are you?"

"I am Seng Shan."

"I remember hearing about you before the Last War. -- A Shaolin Monk who left the Temple in China to spread kung fu to America. I thought you were dead by now."

"Apparently not," the monk replied in a sarcastic tone.

"You're going to make swords like this for me," Abraham said, as he twirled the weapon in his hand, eyes riveted on the sword.

"I will never make weapons for you," the monk replied in a calm but forceful voice. "I would rather die."

"I am sure you would, old man," Abraham responded with the emphasis on "old man." "But it isn't you who will die if you disobey me."

With a haughty grin, Abraham snapped his fingers. Two demons dragged an older woman and a child from a nearby building, their bodies battered and bruised, legs sliding through cold stone and concrete. The older woman appeared to be about the same age as the monk, her face covered in wrinkles, but an air of dignity was easily noticeable even under the circumstances. The young boy couldn't have been more than ten, his dark black hair a tangled mess, sprouting out in every direction from his plump, round face. They were both of Asian descent.

"Who do we have here?" Abraham asked the woman and boy.

Neither of them responded, so Abraham turned back to the monk and said with a snicker, "I see a resemblance. Could they be related to you?"

The monk said nothing.

"Put a knife to the old woman's throat," Abraham commanded one of his demons, and then he turned back to Seng Shan and said, "I'll ask you one last time. Will you make swords for me?"

The monk didn't reply immediately, so Abraham nodded toward the demon holding the old woman, and the creature slit her throat. The blood gushed out, and she crumpled lifelessly to the ground.

"No!" Seng Shan screamed, dropping his shoulders and slipping free from the two demons holding him. Even at his advanced age, he burst forward, lunging the few remaining feet that separated him and Abraham. Expecting the attack, Abe still sitting on his steed, he kicked out with his left leg, sending the monk sprawling back into the arms of several demons. This time the creatures tied the monk's hands behind his back.

With an air of pomposity, Abraham dismounted and sauntered up to Seng Shan as the demons held the monk in place. Abe smiled, grabbed the monk by the face, looked into his eyes, and said, "The woman was too old to serve any purpose in the slave camps. You, on the other hand, will build me enough swords for an army, or I will kill the boy. Do you understand?"

Seng Shan glared at him, eyes blazing, with spittle dripping from his lips, "I understand completely."

Abraham's thoughts returned to the present as he approached the armory in Houston. Before the war, the building was a machine shop used to build molds for the automotive industry. As Abraham entered, he could see milling machines, lathes, and grinders stretched from wall to wall. Unfortunately, these couldn't be used anymore, due to the lack of electricity.

Nonetheless, there were several workstations set up in the middle of the factory, along with furnaces nearby. Humans pounded away with their hammers at every worktable, their bodies glistening with sweat, as a light breeze blew through the large open doors, sending the stifling heat in like it was the breath of hell. Others grabbed the worked steel with tongs and placed it into the hot furnaces, removing it and dipping it into buckets of water, causing the sizzling whistle of steam as it screamed out in defiance. Over and over this action was repeated, minutes turning into hours, as the forged metal transformed into weapons of death.

Seng Shan was at the far end of the building overseeing production. Abraham rode his steed down the center aisle until he reached the monk.

"I need one hundred swords immediately."

"They're in the storage room," the monk replied with contempt in his voice.

"How many swords are completely finished?" Abraham commanded.

"Two hundred and thirty."

"Good, make sure the quota for this week is completed."

As Abraham headed to the storage room to inspect the weapons, he could feel the monk's eyes boring through the back of his head. Hate could be a dangerous thing, but he knew the monk would perform his duties. He wouldn't risk his grandson's life.

He Speaks

Seeing HIM do so many things through the years, you would think nothing he could do would impress me any longer. There were many stories about the miracles humans had performed before the Last War. Some people thought that maybe humans had become God–like. I wondered now if the man I traveled with could be part God, for that day, I saw him do the impossible. No man could make that shot unless he were a God, or God himself had come down from the Heavens and guided the arrow.

The arrow traveled as fast as a lightning bolt, covering the distance instantly. The missile never dropped or wavered in its flight. Just as the demon's blade started to descend, the arrow blasted into its head. The impact was so hard that the creature flew back into several other demons behind him, the monster's body landing in a heap, motionless, nearly twenty feet away.

All of it happened so quickly that some of the demons didn't even know what had occurred. They continued their frantic dancing and screaming around what I could now make out was a large fountain. A small girl with brown hair was stretched across it, her arms and legs bound on each end.

As I observed these details, three things happened at once. First off, we had covered more distance. Second, our dark companion had already notched, drawn, and fired another arrow. Lastly, at the same time, all the demons finally realized that something was amiss.

The arrow took another demon down, and then our dark

friend abandoned the bow for his swords. With his horse still moving at full speed, he swung his leg over the steed's back, jumped to the ground, rolled forward on his shoulder, and leaped to his feet. Some of the demons were so mesmerized by the shocking turn of events that they put up no resistance as my dark companion began his magical dance of death.

One of the demons stood frozen, a mask of stupidity plastered on its face. The next second, the top portion of the creature's face slid off diagonally from where the sword had made its cut. For just a moment, the remaining eye attempted to look in the direction of its missing face before the demon crumbled to the dirt.

Three other demons tried to rush our friend all at once, figuring they would overpower him. Instead, they found all their legs removed from the knee down as he dropped low, spun on one knee, and brought his swords in a circular motion.

Five more remained, and the creatures tried to be more cautious, pulling out their clubs and waiting for the man to come to them. But every time they swung their weapons, the dark warrior sidestepped, ignoring the attack and simply cutting their hands off at the wrist. They screamed in agony, blood squirting everywhere as their clubs still clutched in the lifeless hands dropped to the ground. Fortunately for them, the pain didn't last long, as our companion continued his momentum, spinning behind the monsters and following up with devastating swings to their necks, toppling their heads from their bodies.

All of this happened so fast that Bill and I didn't even have time to join the fray. By the time we dismounted our horses, our dark companion had already cut the young girl's bonds, freeing her from the fountain. She immediately ran several yards to our left, abruptly coming to a halt.

Frozen except for a slight twitch in her hands, the young girl's eyes remained fixated on the most gruesome scene I had ever witnessed. A woman's body lay on the ground, but her arms and legs were removed, lying in the dirt a few feet away. You could tell that they had been pulled off. If they had been cut, you would see a smooth separation, but the flesh and tendons were unevenly torn. Some veins and arteries were still connected, hanging on like long spider webs, stretched from the body to the limbs.

The worst part was her stomach. It looked like someone had dug her abs out with a shovel. A huge bloody hole remained, and her intestines were strung out across the ground, like some kind of sick net of evil, waiting to capture its victim.

A few feet away was the body of a man in the same condition, except for the stomach. This hadn't been touched; however, his head had been removed and lay several yards away standing upright, eyes open, looking back at us from the final moment of his existence.

The girl just stood there staring, locked in a glacier of misery. These must have been her parents, and I could only imagine the sorrow she was feeling. She wasn't crying, so I assumed she was probably in shock.

My heart melted when I looked at her heart-shaped face, beautiful brown hair, and those bright blue eyes. Even though she was caked in dirt, and her clothes were nothing but torn rags, I observed a certain dignity combined with serenity. Something seemed so familiar. I feel like I've seen her before, but I can't quite place it. Where had she come from?

There is something I neglected to tell you earlier. I have no memory of anything that happened before five years ago. I can't remember anything before the day I met HIM. Some traumatic accident or incident must have wiped my memory, and seeing this little girl made me think that perhaps I had met her long ago, but I realized she would have only been a baby at that time. Maybe she reminded me of someone else.

"Sweetheart, what's your name?" I quietly asked, but she gave me no response.

"She's in shock," Bill replied. "It's weird. I feel like I've seen her before."

"I feel the same way. Where do we know her from?"

Looking around the village, we hoped that someone else could give us the answers about this mysterious little girl, but all the humans had fled into hiding as soon as we attacked the demons. From the looks of us, they probably didn't know if we were friends or foe. We couldn't blame them. It was hard to trust anyone in this crazy world of ours.

This wasn't the first time we had saved a village from demons, and normally we would have just moved on without a backward glance, but something nagged at me as I looked at this little girl.

Bill must have felt it also because he turned to me and said, "I don't know what it is, but there's something special about her. I can feel it in my bones."

"You're right," I said and turned toward our dark friend. "We need to take her with us."

As usual, I expected the big guy to ignore us, but instead, he walked over, picked her up, and said four simple words, "She'll ride with me."

My jaw dropped, and I looked at Bill to see the exact same reaction. After five long years, our dark companion had finally spoken.

Seng Shan

Seng Shan imagined one of his swords driving through the back of Abraham's head. Every day since the murder of his wife, he dreamed of killing Abraham. Hatred shouldn't control a monk, but he couldn't help it. Controlling his emotions made him remember the old lessons he had learned in China from the Abbot when he was a child.

Young Leung Meng ran down the street, weaving his way through the congestion. Hundreds of people littered the area, moving in a state of tranquility as they practiced their morning routine of tai chi. The boy didn't mean to be disrespectful, but he was running late and needed to make up time. Zigging and zagging like a football player who just received a punt, he jumped over practitioners, crouched in low stances, breaking their concentration, and earning him their resentment. Meng would have to beg for their forgiveness later as he made his way toward his final destination, the Shaolin Temple.

In the background, the boy could see the Songshan Mountain rising high into the clouds. Mount Song is a mountain in central China's Henan Province, along the southern bank of the Yellow River. Meng could make out the lush forests surrounding the mountains, bringing back memories of the endless hours he had spent there practicing kung fu under the canopy of overhanging branches.

Meng had been studying kung fu for as long as he could remember. His father was a Shifu of Ying Jow Fan Zi Mun, (Eagle

Claw somersault boxing) and owned a famous school only a few blocks down the street from the temple. Meng's father had exclusively taught him his style and expected the boy to take over the school one day. Meng loved his father and the Eagle Claw system, but like many other boys from his community, he dreamed of becoming a monk at the Shaolin Temple. However, his father understood and supported his decision. After all, it was a supreme honor to become a monk, and very few martial artists were ever accepted to this prestigious level.

The boy had been coming every morning to the Shaolin Temple for three straight years. Every day the Abbot would test the students to see if they were worthy of becoming a monk. Every time he had come close to being accepted, he had failed. Gritting his teeth, the boy thought, *today will be different*.

Entering the training area on the front side of the temple, he started warming up with the other students, stretching his body and contorting it into positions that most Olympic gymnasts would find impossible to duplicate.

Within a few minutes, the creek of heavy doors entered his ears, and he knew that Abbot Hao had entered the practice area. The Abbot was the Grandmaster of the Temple and had held this position for longer than Meng had been alive. He had the final say on what students would be accepted to become a monk, so everyone sprung to attention when the Abbot commanded them to line up.

For almost a minute, the Abbot walked up and down the line, steps as quiet as a cat's paws and his glare as intent as an eagle's eyes. Meng knew he was reading the prospective students, staring into their eyes, determining who was worthy.

"Mabu!" the Abbot shouted in an earth-rattling cry.

Everyone dropped low into a horse stance. The position must be perfect, or they would immediately tell them to leave. Their thighs must remain level to the ground, backs as straight as an arrow. Feet must point straight ahead, hands remaining fists, tight in the chambers above the hip bone. If anyone made the slightest movement, the Abbot would dismiss them.

Back and forth, Abbot Hao walked the rows in between the students, his orange robes fluttering in the wind. Several minutes passed, and young Meng could feel the sweat pouring down his face as his legs began to burn in agony. With his peripheral vision, he could see some of the other students breaking position and being told to leave, but he refused to be dismissed. He continued holding the horse stance for what seemed like an eternity, muscles cramping, pin-pricks dancing across his thighs like an evil ballerina intent on driving him insane.

Legend said that a monk never felt pain and could hold a low stance for hours without moving. Meng had never been able to hold it longer than ten minutes, but that was still longer than most of the other students who wanted to be disciples. Regardless, he knew the Abbot would only accept one student this year, and this would be the final test. *I won't give up.*

"Your Mabu must be strong just like a mountain is strong," said the Abbot to the remaining students. "The problem is you let your bodies control your minds. Free your mind of pain. Free your mind of emotion. Your body should be like a mountain. Does a mountain cry?"

"No, Da Shifu!" the students shouted in unison.

"Does a mountain hate?"

"No, Da Shifu!"

"Does a mountain feel pain?"

"No, Da Shifu!"

"Clear your minds and become the mountain."

Seng Shan remembered how he felt that day when he learned how to clear his mind and block out the pain. It wasn't just physical pain, but mental and emotional pain also. His mind drifted away into another world. This world felt warm. It felt safe. Joy took hold of his being instead of pain. The forests he had trained in ever since he was a young child took form, their leaves blowing in the soft breeze. The breeze invaded his senses, bringing him the song of chirping birds and the smell of moist grass.

Most of all, he could feel Song Mountain pulsing with all its majestic power, like a giant king who had fallen in battle eons ago. Its peaks were wearing a crown of ice that once ruled kingdoms. Its waterfalls, and rivers flowing through its rocky outcrops, were the arteries and veins of this mighty and fallen hero of old.

That day almost eighty years ago, he was still holding horse stance when the Abbot commanded him to rise. Lost in meditation for so long, he hadn't realized that all the other students had been dismissed. When he had begun his meditation, it was early morning, but now he realized the sun was already fading over the horizon. He was accepted that day as a disciple of Shaolin and given his religious name. Seng Shan means Monk of the Mountain.

Seng Shan breathed in and returned his thoughts to the present. Pushing his hatred aside, he gained control of his emotions. Revenge would come in time, but he had a task to perform.

A demon kept watch over the armory, but like clockwork, he fell asleep every day during this time. Over the last few months, Seng Shan had started teaching the workers Chinese, so if the demon awoke, he wouldn't know what they were saying. One of the workers raised his arm and nodded toward the demon, giving him the signal that the creature was sound asleep. The workers continued pounding away on the steel, but as they did, Seng Shan shouted out his commands in Chinese.

"Everyone, Mabu stance!"

"Yes, Da Shifu!" all the workers shouted in unison as they dropped into position.

"Your legs will become as strong as the steel you forge!"

the monk shouted. “This will make you move faster, jump higher, and kick harder! Do you understand?!”

“Yes, Da Shifu!”

“Does steel feel pain?”

“No, Da Shifu!”

“Does steel feel emotion?”

“No, Da Shifu!”

“Then clear your minds and become steel! Clear your minds and make yourself into the weapon you were meant to be!”

The Dream

"What the hell is going on?" Bill exclaimed with a look of puzzlement on his face.

"I don't know," I replied. "I'm as shocked as you are."

"All this time, I thought he might have been freaking mute."

"That crossed my mind also."

"It's got to be the girl. I told you she was special."

Bill was right, but I just couldn't put my finger on it. What was so special about her? We both felt like we had seen her before, but where? Maybe she had been in another village we had traveled through previously, but that would be nearly impossible. Very few people owned horses these days, and I highly doubted she could have passed us on foot.

Even if we had seen her before, what difference did that make to the big guy? We had seen plenty of kids over the last few years, and he never showed interest in any of them. Why would he take her with him, and what had caused him to speak? Taking her with us just put her in danger. We were demon hunters, and the last thing we needed was a little girl to protect. But somehow, deep in my bones, I knew she had to go with us. We had no other choice, but I couldn't explain it. I had to find out more.

Our dark leader and the little girl were already leaving the village when I caught up to them.

"Hey, big guy, how are you doing?"

Our solemn friend made no response and just continued riding forward.

"Is everything okay?" I asked a little louder to make sure he could hear me.

Again, there was no response from our dark companion.

"I guess he's back to playing mute again," Bill chuckled.

If he wasn't going to respond, maybe the girl could shine some light on our new situation. She still looked like she was in shock, sitting there staring straight ahead, eyes unblinking like she was unaware of anyone or anything.

"What's your name, princess?"

Again, I received no response, but I pushed further.

"Are you hungry?"

Only a blank look stared back at me.

I was about to give up when Bill and I were thrown astray for the second time today.

"Are you hungry?" our dark leader asked her.

The little girl nodded yes in response, so he reached into his pouch and pulled out a piece of boar meat. Tearing off a small slice, he handed it to the girl. Hands darting forward, she grabbed the food and started devouring it like she hadn't eaten in weeks. While this occurred, Bill and I exchanged looks, not knowing what to say. --- Finally, Bill couldn't hold it in any longer.

"What the hell! I'm tired of this crap! For all these years, we have stuck by you, and not once did you have the decency to give us a peep. Now, this girl pops into the picture, and suddenly you remember how to work your mouth. Tell us what the hell is going on, or I'm going to kick your ass!"

With that, the big guy quickly turned his head and deeply stared at Bill.

Bill met that penetrating gaze, swallowed, fumbled his words, and said in a much softer tone, "Well - - - I mean - - - I know you'll kill me, but I would appreciate some kind of response."

"She rides with us, and that is all you need to know," our dark friend replied as he continued looking at Bill with those cold, piercing eyes.

Bill knew his threat had crossed a line, but I doubt our dark friend had actually taken it seriously. Bill gulped in his throat, then turned to me and said, "I think I have all the information I need."

"I figured you would say that," I responded with a knowing smile.

"I almost crapped my pants. I think I liked it better when he didn't talk."

Silently, we continued heading south on path 45 for the next two hours, our eyelids growing heavy as nightfall approached. We found a suitable place to camp for the night, out in the open where lurking eyes would have a hard time sneaking up on us without being seen.

After preparations were finished, we started a fire and made dinner. Of course, boar meat would be the entrée, but we also had a jar of honey for special occasions. Bill and I thought our new guest would enjoy this treat, and we weren't disappointed. She gulped it down voraciously, and I soon saw her disconnection return to normal. She still didn't feel like talking, but the zombie-like look was gone, and we noticed her eyes scanning the area.

A necklace dangled on the young girl's chest, and I noticed something engraved on it. Our leader must have seen it at the same time because he said to her, "What does it say on your necklace?" She didn't respond but instead pulled it out and showed it to him.

"Angelica, is that your name?"

Once again, she didn't speak but nodded yes.

"Well, at least we know her name," Bill said.

Bill and I tried to ask her a few more questions, but she wouldn't answer us. Then we saw her eyelids starting to close, and we realized how tired she must be. The big guy laid her down with a gentleness I didn't think he possessed and covered her with a blanket. Within a few seconds, she was sound asleep, soft snores slipping away from her mouth and nostrils. The stress of losing her parents must have taken a toll on the girl, and sleep was probably the best medicine.

Not remembering my parents, I could only imagine the pain Angelica was going through. Her story was very similar to our dark friend's. They had both lost the closest people in their lives and maybe that was their connection. Perhaps that was the reason he had taken her. He sympathized with her loss because it reminded him of his own grief.

Tears swelling in my eyes, I glanced at him, and then I looked back at Angelica. Our friend's pain had turned him into a killing machine that was totally devoid of emotion, a man that until now hadn't spoken a single word to another human being in over five years. What would Angelica's pain do to her? Would it change her into something else? I added these questions to my journal, along with the rest of the day's adventure, and put the book away.

Bill and I were both getting tired, so we decided to lie down for the night. Before I closed my eyes, I remembered looking at sweet Angelica and thinking how innocent she was. She deserved so much better. She was so much better...

Angelica was laughing. I was tickling her, and she screamed out in glee. Her laugh was the most beautiful thing I had ever heard.

A child's laugh was so precious. No matter how bad your day was, a child's laugh could always turn things around. We were in a small room maybe ten feet wide by ten feet long with two beds against the far wall, and the one Angelica stood on was full of stuffed animals. The room was plain with peaceful walls and a grey concrete floor, and it was immaculate. The bedsheets were tucked in so tight that they gave off a military vibe. A few pictures were hung with precision on the walls, but as hard as I tried, I couldn't focus on them. It felt like something was preventing me from seeing them. That's okay, why look at pictures when I can look at Angelica? Her hair was combed and tied in two ponytails. She was wearing dark jeans accompanied by a tee-shirt, and I think the shirt said something like Amberhobbi. My hands were around her tiny waist, easily lifting her in the air. I tossed her up, being careful that my throw wasn't high enough to hit the ceiling. She screamed out with joy, but as she fell back into my hands, I realized she was much lighter. I tossed her again, and each time she seemed to shrink in size. She wasn't just getting smaller; she was getting younger. Every time I thought this was strange, I looked into her pretty blue eyes, and all my curiosities floated away. She transformed into a toddler, giggling like crazy, making me laugh even harder. My nostrils inhaled that soft baby smell. It smelled like happiness, and it was contagious. I don't think I've ever felt so happy. One more time, I tossed her in the air, hands ready to catch her and save her from injury. --- I kept waiting, but she never came down, --- she was gone.

I felt the darkness overtake me, screams rattling through the air over and over, and then I realized I was screaming too. Nothing could be this painful, and I had to escape from this misery. I tried to run away, but I couldn't move. My feet were cemented to the floor. I felt the pain slowly creeping through my body, and there was nothing I could do to stop it. It started in my stomach and wound its way upward like a snake, strangling my soul. My mind was on fire, burning to the point of explosion. The snake crawled into my throat, digging a hole into my brain. I must bury this pain away and never let it return. I screamed for the last time.

Jumping up from my bedroll, perspiration dripping down my face, I realized my whole body was covered in sweat. Breathing heavily, heart racing, I covered my mouth, dry heaving like my stomach was trying to jump out of my throat. The pain I experienced in my nightmare still lingered, causing me to glare at Angelica. Her chest rose up and down under the blanket, the sounds of snoring telling me she was fine. My pain faded away, and my body returned to normal.

"Wow, you had one hell of a wet dream," Bill joked. "Did you bang an entire village of Amazon woman? That's the dream I have every night."

"I don't know what kind of dream that was, but I don't ever want to feel like that again," I replied.

Tiredness outweighed my anxieties, so I went back to bed, and luckily, the remainder of the night was dreamless. I woke the next morning feeling refreshed. We packed up and started our never-ending journey toward Hus – town. At least it felt never-ending. We had been traveling this way for so long that it almost seemed unreal our destination was finally within reach. Why does time seem to slow down the closer you get to your goal?

As the day passed, we traveled through the remains of a few villages. It seemed the closer we came to Hus – town, the fewer standing structures appeared. Everything seemed devastated, barren wastelands as far as the eye could see. On both sides of the path, hundreds of signs were bent like an old man's back, his vertebrae creaking in the wind as he nudges closer to his final days.

We had just approached a small bridge labeled number 8 that crossed over path 45 when we detected motion in the distance. Ahead, we could see dust rising in the air and heard a loud noise heading in our direction.

Our group moved off the path to hide as our dark companion scaled the embankment next to the bridge so he could ascertain a better view. He came down a short time later and spoke to Angelica, "Stay with them, no matter what happens."

The young girl glanced in our direction with a confused look on her face. Frightened, she tried to grab at the big guy, but he pushed her arm away. Then he mounted his horse and took off down the path.

Bill, Angelica, and I climbed the embankment so we could see for ourselves what our dark friend had seen. Peering from atop the hill, our dark friend emerged on the other side of the bridge, riding forward without a care in the world as he crossed the field toward them. In the distance, a human sat mounted on a horse, an army of demons formed ranks behind him, their weapons ready for battle. There must have been at least five hundred of them.

The Battle At Beltway 8

Abraham commanded one hundred demons to gather swords from the armory and follow him north. As they marched up Interstate 45, he sent other demons ahead to recruit more followers. Soon their numbers swelled to nearly five hundred. Abe wanted to see if this mysterious rider was as powerful as he had heard. If needed, he would test the man's prowess with overwhelming numbers and the new swords created by Seng Shan.

A gigantic smile crossed Abraham's face. As a child, he never could have imagined being the leader of an army. He had always been a weak little follower, but now he was looked up to, and it felt good to wield that power. The humans feared him and obeyed his every command. That is if you could still call them human.

The slaves they captured called them demons, and that name was fitting. The radiation poisoning had eaten away at their bodies and warped their minds. After the nuclear blast, they shambled around aimlessly, writhing in pain and contemplating suicide. Most would have died within days, but then the Master saved them.

Travelling through the rubble of Houston, the Master found them and blessed their crippled bodies with his touch. He laid his beautiful hand on their heads, granting them mercy, removing their pain, and showing them the way to return their senses. He gave them a wondrous purpose. They would have the chance to represent him and spread his beliefs across the world. A new world would be formed in his image. Abraham touched his chest and breathed in, feeling the excitement build within him, for he would be a pivotal part of this new world order. *How did I get so lucky?*

The army passed interstate 610, almost reaching Tidwell Road. Hundreds of slaves were working on both sides of the expressway, erecting new structures. The crack of the whip could be heard the closer he approached, making Abraham's smile spread even farther. The demon leaders pushed the arrogant slaves to their limits, and Abe enjoyed every minute of their displeasure. *A new world will be built for the glory of the Master, and pain will pave the way.*

Suddenly, to his left, he sensed some commotion. Darting his eyes in that direction, he saw a man running away from his taskmasters, leaving the construction site, and entering the open wastelands. Several demons were in hot pursuit, screaming for him to halt and throwing their clubs, hoping to knock the man unconscious or at least cause him to fall. Just when it looked like he might escape, one of the clubs missed the man's legs but landed directly in front of his feet. The slave stumbled, falling face-first into the dirt. In an instant, the demons were upon him, kicking and punching until the man was a bloody pulp. Tying a rope around his feet, they dragged him back to the other slaves.

Abraham thought, *how foolish to think you could escape. A mere slave will never have any control or say in this new world the Master is creating. People are so arrogant. So many had thought they were in control because of personal wealth. They stuck their noses up in the air, in all their haughtiness, and thought money guaranteed them respect. Doctors, lawyers, and movie stars all died the same way when the nukes hit. Money and fame didn't save them. I rose to a higher position than anyone when the earth was cleansed. Money didn't make me the man I am, obedience did. The Master has shown me the way to true power, and now I wield it in his blessed name.*

The demon army continued their march for several hours, stopping once for a brief rest and a quick meal. They had almost reached Beltway 8 when Abraham saw a single human rider coming toward them in the distance. Abe already knew it had to be the warrior he sought, for no one else would dare approach an army of demons with a total disregard of fear. Abraham badly wanted to attack so he could test his new weapons and show the warrior who was in control. However, he remembered what the Master had told him about bringing the warrior to him unmolested, and halfheartedly, he commanded his army to stand down. He would have to wait and see how this played out.

Slowly trotting up, the rider pulled the reigns on his steed, stopping the beast approximately thirty feet from Abraham. Abraham could see the man was dressed in black, with two swords strapped to each side of his waist. It was hard to tell how tall he was, with him sitting on top of a horse, but Abe guessed he was slightly bigger than the average man. He had piercing eyes and a rugged look, but there was definitely nothing supernatural about his appearance.

"I am Abraham. What is your name?"

The dark figure said nothing. He just sat there on his horse, staring ahead with those dark, cold eyes.

Raising his voice, Abraham said, "My Master would like to meet you. He has sent us to escort you to him. Remove your weapons and come peacefully, or face the consequences."

"The only consequence will be your death, but I will save you for last, so the fear can mount as your army diminishes before you," the dark figure responded in a calm, calculating voice.

As soon as the last syllable left the dark figure's tongue, he attacked. Abraham watched in awe as this man moved faster than anything he had ever seen. Pulling out his bow, he notched an arrow and fired, all in one motion. It seemed as soon as one arrow hit its mark; another was already being released. Before Abraham could even give the command to attack, five of his soldiers lay dead.

"The Master commanded to take him alive!" Abraham screamed wide-eyed as he bit his lower lip. "Surround him and use your numbers to overwhelm him!"

Frozen, except for his hands which ground together as the sweat grew in his palms, Abraham couldn't believe what his eyes were showing him. Before his soldiers could surround the dark warrior, the man had already launched all his arrows. Twenty of his demons lay dead or in the final throes of death, moaning, and blood gurgling from their mouths.

Then the mighty warrior spurred his horse forward, charging straight at the army like a tank. Horse and man plowed into the horde, swords hacking away, leaving a trail of blood behind them. The weapons moved so fast that it was nearly impossible to see them. The only time they appeared to be briefly discernible was when they entered a body. The bone and flesh slowing them down for a split second until the weapon was removed.

The horse smashed through the army, scattering demons like they were bowling ball pins. Some of the beasts stayed farther away, stabbing with their spears, but every time they would thrust from one side, the man would hop down to the opposite side, still holding on to the saddle with one hand and using his sword to hack through demons on that side. Then with one agile move, he would jump back into the saddle and continue his onslaught forward.

Abraham's grinding hands had spread to his arms. The appendages shook like he was having a seizure as sweat filled his armpits. His strategy wasn't working. Over a hundred of his warriors were already dead. *Do something, you idiot! --- You'll never capture him as long as the horse lives.*

"Forget the warrior! Kill the horse!" he screamed at the top of his lungs.

The demons started to attack the horse by whatever means possible. They thrust with their spears, swung with their clubs, and even threw rocks at the beast. The warrior swung his swords with blinding speed, deflecting the projectiles with pinpoint accuracy. Nevertheless, even his amazing skill couldn't stop everything. Little by little, strikes found their mark, digging deeply into the animal.

"Take its legs out!" Abraham shouted with glee as he saw his plan starting to work.

While demons were attacking from both sides, several others charged from the front with the new swords made by Seng Shan. Just when they were about to strike the horse's legs, the dark warrior gave a command, and the beast jumped upward, sharpened weapons slicing harmlessly beneath the animal.

For a moment, man and horse became one being, soaring and rising above the turmoil, but then they came down on uneven ground, the horse's right leg landing awkwardly with a resounding pop as its front leg snapped. The dark warrior was thrown forward, but his concentration remained focused as he dived through the air, extended his swords, cut the throats of two demons, tucked and rolled, and was up fighting once again.

Abraham couldn't help but admire the phenomenal skill of this dark warrior. Every time his soldiers tried to rush in, they were met with steel. Blood and bodies were everywhere, but instead of this being an impediment for the man, he used it to his advantage. As demons attempted to bull rush him, they would slip on the blood, fall to the ground, and trip the others pushing from behind.

One time, it seemed that they almost had him by the sheer numbers crowding in, but then the warrior turned, ran, and leaped over a pile of dead bodies that had to be at least five feet high. By the time the demons got around the obstacle, he had already cut a path of death through several more monsters.

On another occasion, one of the demons stabbed its spear toward the warrior's leg. The man blocked down crossing his swords, and then in one fluid movement, he twisted, lifting the weapon up and over his head, separating his arms, and turning quickly to yank the weapon from the creature's grasp. Holding the spear between his swords and behind his back, like a crucifixion, he spun and let the weapon fly, finding its mark in a demon's face.

Instantly the warrior was up again and sprinting into the horde, sliding from side to side like a skater on the bloody field, both swords moving in a figure-eight motion, cutting out a corridor of both flesh and fear as demons tried to flee but could find no recourse but death.

Abraham had lost track, but he could tell hundreds of his soldiers had already died or lay wounded. However, besides the attempted attack on the dark warrior's horse, he had kept his soldiers with the new, improved weapons made by the monk in the rear. He thought that maybe they wouldn't be necessary, but now he saw they would be his only hope.

"Surround him and move in slowly with blades forward!" Abraham commanded his new elite guard.

The demons did as they were told, forming a wall of steel around the dark warrior. In unison, they took one step forward at a time, shoulder to shoulder, swords pointed ahead like spears.

Rather than waiting until the circle was too small to retreat, the warrior moved forward and attacked the demons to his left, swinging his swords forcefully with the tips pointing down, hoping to knock several blades aside and create a path to escape.

The swords moved so quickly that Abraham couldn't even see the movement, but he could hear the sound, and it brought a smile to his face. When steel breaks, it makes a distinctive ringing pop, and that is the noise that entered Abe's ears. One second the dark warrior held two powerful swords. A moment later, he backed away, only holding two hilts in his hands.

Exhaling through pursed lips and wiping the sweat from his brow, Abraham shouted to the warrior, "You have fought bravely. The Master honors you by giving you the privilege of meeting him. Surrender, and your life will be spared."

Defiantly, the dark warrior glared at him and gave his response by dropping into a cross-legged position; arms spread out behind his back like wings. Abraham could see that his hands formed a clutching position and recognized the stance from old kung fu movies. *The Eagle Claw style.*

The warrior shot up from his stance like a loaded spring, running to his right, arms spread out behind him. Just before he hit the wall of demons, he seemed to rise, but it was only a ruse. As the monsters lifted their swords upward, anticipating the warrior would jump over them, he quickly dropped and slid through one of their legs. Passing beneath the creature, his claw-like hand clamped on the demon's groin and ripped it from its body. The beast dropped screaming in agony, clutching the open hole between his legs that now gushed a river of blood. Pandemonium broke out in the demon ranks.

Behind the wall of swords, the warrior still faced more than a hundred demons, but these only carried crude spears or clubs. Many of them tried to escape, stumbling over their brethren, but they weren't fast enough to avoid extinction.

Abraham had thought Seng Shan moved with speed and precision, but this man gave unarmed combat a totally new meaning. Actually, unarmed combat didn't seem an accurate description. The warrior's hands seemed to be steel, vise-like weapons, causing havoc everywhere they went. Sometimes he would sidestep with blazing speed, avoiding a knife thrust, grab the wrist with one hand digging into vital pressure points, and with the other hand, he would tear his opponent's throat out. Other times he would make the same catch of the wrist, but instead of attacking the throat, he would thrust his arm in a chopping motion, using his forearm bone to strike above his victim's elbow. The result would be painful screams as a demon's arm was snapped in half.

With obliteration facing his army, Abraham thought, *I need to get things under control.* As the warrior was creating a field of carnage, he once again commanded his elite guard to encircle the battlefield. They started to move in unison, but this time he warned them to keep their swords straight ahead and not move them no matter what happened. They started their slow march, one step at a time, forcing the regular demons to continue fighting or die on the blades of the Elite Guard.

Abraham pushed up from his saddle, locking his legs and straining his eyes for a better view. The demon bodies were piled so high they could no longer fall to the ground. Each time they died, they would either collapse to a kneeling position or even stand, propped up by the wall of demons behind them. The elite guard kept moving in step by step, pushing the dead bodies in front of them.

Finally, Abraham saw the warrior's head pop up from a mountain of corpses. The man tried to climb out, but he kept slipping on the blood and sweat of his victims. *They have to stop him before he breaks free.*

"Grab him! Make sure he doesn't escape!" Abraham shouted as he clapped his hands together with joy.

The Elite Guard attempted to crawl up the mound of the dead, slipping and sliding on blood and loose body parts. It became a race as the warrior continued to squirm out to waist level, and the Elite Guard plunged their swords into demon bodies, using the weapons as hooks to drag themselves to the top. The warrior was almost out, and Abraham nibbled at his lip, sweat and shakes attacking his mind and body. Just when it looked like he might escape, the man slipped back down to his waist, and the demons were upon him.

Even without the use of his legs, the warrior could still cause devastation. As one demon tried to grab him, he blocked and drove his hardened fingers into its eyes. Another demon attempted to grab him from the left, but he yanked the creature forward, smashing his head into the monster's face, breaking its nose.

Unfortunately, the warrior couldn't turn, and the demons that had climbed the pile to his back were able to grab his arms. The warrior shook his body, twisting and turning, hoping to escape their grip, but more demons joined the skirmish, and they were finally able to tie his arms behind his back. Pulling him from the pile, the creatures dragged him unceremoniously across the ground, dropping him at Abraham's feet.

Breathing a sigh of relief, Abraham glanced down at the magnificent warrior before him. Out of the nearly five-hundred demons he had brought with him, fewer than one hundred remained alive. If it weren't for the new swords, they all would have died. *He was right when he said my fear would mount as I watched the army dwindle. I was afraid for the first time in many years, but I can't let anyone see it.*

"So, you said you would kill me last." Abraham defiantly stated. "I'm still here."

The warrior scowled up at him and replied, "The day isn't over yet."

The demons tied the warrior to the back of Abraham's horse and started their march back to Houston. The Master would be waiting…

Him

I'm going to kill them all! Whatever it takes, I will wipe them from the planet! Their life force will fade away as I peer into their eyes and bathe in their blood! This fool, Abraham, will feel my blades dig deep into his body, but I will take my time with this one. I will make him suffer, just like they made them ------ suffer. No!!! Don't think about that! Push it away. Push it away. My head is pounding! My blood is on fire! My heart feels like it is being squeezed in a vise! Breathe and control this rage that consumes me, or I'll lose them and slip into darkness forever. I've just started to wake up from the nightmare. I can't return. Focus on Angelica's face and remember that she is safe with my friends.

Breathing in through my nose and out through my mouth, I feel the fires subside, and a semblance of clarity returns. My arms are bound behind me, and no matter how hard I try, I can't break them. Abraham rides in front of me, and what is left of the demon army surrounds me, but they keep their distance. I can feel their fear, and it gives me great pleasure. If I could only break free, I would destroy all of them! I'll cut through their flesh like butter! I'll snap their bones and tear their skin off! I'll --- wait! Calm down, stupid. You can't lose control. Angelica is safe, so everything is okay. If she is unharmed, then the dark rage inside me will dissipate.

Why have I felt this way ever since I first saw her? I feel like I've come out of an endless sleep, and for the first time, I can remember pieces of my past. For so long, all I felt is death. It almost seems as if death is alive and that he is me. It is all I have seen, and it is all

I have known. From the time I wake each morning until the time I go to bed, all I think about is killing. I would thirst for death like someone dying of dehydration. I would hunger for it like someone who is starving.

And then I saw her, and everything changed. Her hair, her eyes, the shape of her face bring me peace. The way she talks, the way she walks, reminds me of something. Argh, why can't I remember? When I try to think about it, I feel a sense of lingering pain rising up, forcing my memories away. Who am I, and what's happening to me? --- The only thing I know for sure is that I must protect Angelica. Nothing else matters.

Thankfully, she is safe. I can sense my friends with her, over at the battlefield. Why would they go there? Maybe they're scavenging the bodies, looking for supplies. That's good thinking. They must be stocking up before they leave for someplace safe. My friends will find a town where they can settle down, and maybe Bill will finally find a woman and get laid. That's all that moron ever talks about.

Yeah, I feel much better. For the first time in as long as I can remember, I feel happy. Pleasure is something I've only felt when I kill, but this is something totally different. Angelica has unlocked something inside of me that has been hidden for so many years. I sense another side to me that I didn't know existed, or maybe it did exist once. I just can't remember it. Fleeting images of Angelica and someone else enters my mind. The other person is a woman, but I can't focus on her picture. It's like I'm looking through a dirty lens. Even the images of Angelica are confusing. Sometimes I see her as a child, and at other times I remember her being older. Nothing makes sense, but I'm sure I will figure it out eventually. Unfortunately, I'll probably never see her again, but that's okay. If I know she is safe; then I'll be happy.

This piece of scum --- Abraham can kill me whenever he wants, yet he has some plan for me. He said he's taking me to his master, and I hope I get the chance to kill this monster. I hope I get the opportunity to kill all of them. I want them all to die! Revenge will be mine for what they did! Rage is my name! Blood and death are what I bring! ...... Stop you fool! Breathe in, breathe out, in, out. Calm down and get control. Wait --- something doesn't feel right.

Looking over my shoulder again, I see my friends far in the distance. They're following me. Why would those fools follow me? Why are you taking her toward danger instead of away from it? When I get my hands on you idiots, I'll tear you apart! Luckily the demons aren't looking backward. Besides, Angelica is doing her best to stay out of view. She's a smart girl, but she has always been smart. I remember her reading when she was only three --- Wait --- What am I thinking of? That couldn't have been her. She's too young. I try to remember, but the wall comes up again. Everything is so blurry. For an instant, I broke through, but now I can't find my way around it. Every time I try, my head begins to throb, and I feel the darkness retake me. Push it away or I'll lose myself, and this brief glimpse of clarity I've felt will disappear.

We're approaching a village. There are hundreds of humans here and dozens of demons. They are forcing the humans to rebuild the town. It's a slave camp. The humans pour cement and stack bricks as fast as they can, bodies dripping in sweat from the exertion, but it doesn't matter. Regardless of how hard they work, their only reward is pain, as demons crack their whips, push and prod, no matter the output of work. These monsters' need for committing evil has no limits. If only I could free myself, then I would teach them what pain really is.

Abraham stops briefly to talk to one of the demons. From the way he carries himself, this demon must oversee the slave camp.

"How long until the village is finished?" Abraham asked.

"At least six months, sir," the demon replied as he squirmed and bit his lip.

"Six months!"

"Yes, sir," the demon said as he fearfully stepped back. "B— but I'll make sure they finish earlier."

"You better, or I'll grind up your insides and add it to the cement."

"Yes, sir."

The demon backs away, groveling and bowing until he bumps into one of the slaves. The creature turns and cracks a whip on the back of the unsuspecting human. Blood and sorrow are his only reward for a hard day of work.

The army starts to move again. Looking to the rear, I can see my companions moving around the village. Most of the demon's attention is on the slaves, so my friends should be able to pass unnoticed. Why are these idiots following me? What do they think they can accomplish? They're not going to be able to free me. It must be Angelica. Her heart is too big. In one way, I'm upset, but it also pleases me to know she cares. No one has cared about me for a long time. Bill and the other guy have always been there for me, but this is different. I don't know why. --- It just feels --- right.

Don't make your backward glances obvious, stupid. Otherwise, the demons will follow my eyes, and I'll give my friends away. Keep looking in different directions, so they will think it is natural and become used to it. I sneak another peek, but this time I fear my look will surely give them away, as I turn completely around and stare in amazement. They're very far away, but I can see Angelica running toward the village. What is she doing, and why aren't those fools stopping her? The demons will catch her. They will torture her and kill her!

No! The road is moving down an incline, and I can't see them any longer. I stretch my bonds as far as I can. My forearms continue to flex as the sweat pours down my forehead, but nothing happens. The rope is too strong. The uncontrollable rage starts to rise again. I yank at the rope to little avail. It doesn't stop the horse, but it causes Abraham to feel the resistance.

"What are you doing?" Abraham shouts as he turns his steed around and peers at me.

"Argh!" I scream.

The anger consumes me, causing me to lose control and turn back into darkness. Grabbing the rope, I yank at it with all my might and start running from side to side. Abraham is shouting orders, but I cannot hear them. I must escape! I must protect her! Demons come running in, but the fools only bound my hands. The closest demon receives a sidekick to the throat, crushing his windpipe, and he drops to the floor dead. A smile crosses my face.

Two more charge me from opposite directions. One of them dives for my legs. I jump and spin at the same time and the demon that dove misses my jumping leg completely. As I turn in the air, I extend my right leg out, bringing it around like a sideways cartwheel, and drive my heel into the other demon's head. I hear and feel the bones snap --- another smile.

Abraham is shouting again. The demons back off, denying me satisfaction.

"I'll kill all of you! I'm not losing her again! I need to save my dau---!"

"Whack!"

My eyes go blurry, and I feel the pain in the back of my head. I'm falling forward. Everything goes dark...

Angelica's Choice

Utterly amazed, Angelica looked at the scene unfolding in front of her. Thinking back, she couldn't remember what had happened in her village the day before. The shock must have blocked her memory of the events that transpired, but she did know that her parents were dead and that this mighty warrior had saved her life. But she couldn't remember how he had saved her. Watching the battle below, she realized that defeating the small group of demons from her village must have been easy for this incredible man. She didn't think it was possible for anyone to stand against so many demons, but she sensed something very special about this warrior. He must be blessed by God.

She watched the struggle of good versus evil and saw this incredible warrior destroy demons by the hundreds. The tears swelled in her eyes when his horse went down, unable to rise. Then she witnessed the loss of his swords and thought, *he's doomed*. But remarkably, he continued fighting on with unyielding determination.

It was unbelievable how many demons died that day. Their bodies were piled so high that if it weren't for her elevated view, she surely would have lost sight of her liberator. Unfortunately, his good luck couldn't last forever. When the demons climbed the mound of dead behind him, Angelica wanted to scream out a warning, but she doubted he would hear her. Besides, what could one little girl like her do that would change the final outcome?

Angelica watched as the army dragged him away and pondered on her next step of action. The safe course was to return to her town and live out her life hiding from the demons. However, if she did this, her parents would be forgotten, like many others that stood for the side of God. This man had given her hope. God was with him, and he had the power to stop the demon onslaught once and forever. She was only one little girl all by herself, but she had to do something. If it meant her death, then so be it.

Angelica crawled down the embankment and started to follow the demon army. When she reached the battlefield, she came to an abrupt halt. The warrior's horse was lying several yards away, covered in blood, its chest faintly moving up and down. *It's still alive!*

She dashed to the creature, dropping to her knees and inspecting the injury. Its leg had snapped at the knee, bone, and ligaments pointed at an awkward angle. Stroking the animal's face, she gravely looked into its eyes. It was suffering, and she knew she didn't have a choice. Many weapons were lying around the battlefield, so she found a dagger a few feet away and slowly walked back to the horse.

"You helped him destroy those monsters. You should be very proud," Angelica said as the tears streamed down her face.

She had never killed an animal before, but she had seen her father do it. Wiping her eyes, she raised the weapon. Her hand shook as sweat streamed down her arm, but she found the resolve and drove the knife down as hard as she could.

Nose and eyes dripping like an old faucet, Angelica left the battlefield with the knife tucked in her belt. At first, she wanted to throw the weapon away, but then she realized it would serve a better purpose. She would use it to avenge her parents and the horse she was forced to kill. For a second, she almost wiped the blade on her clothes, but she changed her mind. *The blood will intermingle with the demons I kill. This way, the horse will help me do the killing.*

Following the army, the young girl ducked behind broken signs, dead trees, and whatever cover she could find, staying back as far as possible. She was careful to make sure that she could barely see the army in the distance. Every time she lost sight, she would speed up again until they came into view. Diligently, she used this hopping method for the next two hours until the remnants of a village appeared in the distance.

Angelica wasn't sure if this was the demons' final destination, so she would have to be careful. If they posted any sentries, she might be discovered. Crawling on hands and knees, she snuck up closer, creeping up and hiding behind an old steel machine. Her father had told her that before the Last War, these machines could move faster than a horse, but she couldn't comprehend how something without legs could move. Now it was just a piece of burnt-out junk, but it did provide excellent cover.

From her vantage point, she had a clear view of the village and noticed there weren't any sentries. Then again, why would demons need sentries? *They have nothing to fear.* She dashed to the remains of an old building that only had one wall standing.

Looking through an open window, she could see hundreds of people constructing new buildings or repairing the old ones that were salvageable. There were at least a dozen demons holding whips, watching the slaves, and shouting orders. Occasionally, they would strike their whip on the back of one of the humans, leaving scars much deeper than just the flesh. As far as she could tell, they hit their victims for no apparent reason, except for the joy it offered their sick and twisted minds.

In the center of the village, she could see the human who led the demon army talking to a few other demons but couldn't understand what they were saying. Then the man started to move off toward the end of the village, with the demon army and her mysterious friend close behind. She would have to go around the town to remain undetected, and she must move quickly or risk losing them.

Most of the demons kept their focus on the slaves, so it wasn't hard to run from one structure to the next without being seen. Moving quickly, but with soft steps, she had almost made her way completely around the village when screams of a child pierced her ears. A young girl not much older than she was being dragged by a demon into an abandoned house. It wasn't hard to tell what was about to happen. Her parents had warned her about demons raping women and young girls. *I can't let this happen.*

The house was about one hundred feet from her position, but another demon had a clear view of the front door. *Maybe there's a back entrance.* Angelica retraced her steps, finding a different view of the house. From here, she could see that it definitely did have a back door. Digging her feet into the ground, she bolted between the two structures. Gently, she grasped the doorknob, slowly twisting, but it wouldn't budge. The girl screamed from inside the building, and she knew it might already be too late. She peeked around the corner and realized there was no way of getting to the front door without being seen. *What can I do?*

Another scream filled the air, and Angelica started to shake, clenching her fists and digging her nails into her palms. *I have to save this poor girl, regardless if I'm caught.* Panicking, Angelica was about to dash for the front door when she remembered what her parents had taught her – *when all else fails, turn to prayer.*

"Please, God, I need your help?" she desperately whispered.

As soon as she finished her plea, the demon guard turned and started walking in the opposite direction. *Thank you, Lord.* If she was quick, she could still save the little girl. Angelica exploded like a track star, pulled out the knife, and entered the front of the house.

As soon as she entered, her foot caught on a loose piece of tile, and she fell to her knees, losing the grip on her weapon. It clanked to the floor and slid several feet away, stopping halfway between her and the demon. The demon turned at the noise, and Angelica looked up to see the young girl standing behind the demon holding a stick. Apparently, she had been able to use this makeshift weapon to hold the monster off from his advances.

Glancing at the demon, she noticed its soulless white eyes, and then her eyes dropped to the knife on the floor. The creature followed her gaze and then looked back at Angelica. It seemed like time slowed down as they both locked eyes once again. The weapon was closer to the demon, but Angelica had to try for it. Pushing up with her hands, she scrambled across the dirty floor on all fours. The demon was just as quick, diving for the knife at the same time Angelica did. The young girl watched her hand reach out, fingers clawing for the weapon, and thought for sure she would win, but the demon's hand scooped in and tore it away from her at the last second.

With the blade in its hand, the demon spoke in in its gargled speech while glaring down at Angelica, "So, you thought you would come and save your friend. When I'm done with her, you're next."

Angelica's head tilted upward, her vibrant blue eyes finding the lifeless orbs of the monster before her. She thought, do *not forsake me, O Lord.*

The Shelter

It was the middle of the night when Seng Shan rose from his restful sleep. It was the same time he had woken every night for the past few months. He scanned the factory floor, noticing all the workers still peacefully sleeping. There were ninety-three of them under his command, and everyone was loyal to his cause. He had been careful to weed out any possible spies, patiently interrogating each person, pretending to befriend them, and learning their darkest secrets. Everyone in the factory had experienced a tragic loss because of their demon captors, and their hatred far outweighed their fear of death.

Glancing around the room, he saw many young teenagers who weren't much older than his grandson. He knew he would be sending many of these children to their deaths. *Am I doing the right thing? Their blood will be on my hands.*

Abraham had told him that his grandson Fu was being held at the Masters' tower. The man had made it clear that if the quota of swords remained on schedule, Fu would not be harmed. But it had been almost a year since he had seen the young boy, and he wasn't even sure if he was still alive.

Fu was an incredible boy, smart like his mother, and Seng Shan loved him with a passion. Thinking about the boy caused Seng Shan to return to fonder memories from his past.

Shaolin Monks were forbidden to have sex or take a wife, and Seng Shan had remained true to his vows when he lived in China. When he was invited to do the "World Monk Tour," he jumped at the opportunity and visited more than thirty countries. However, out of all the countries he visited, the United States was the one that captured his heart. He asked the Shaolin Temple and received permission to open a Kung Fu school in Houston, Texas.

The school flourished as people not just from Texas but all over the country jumped at the opportunity to learn from an authentic Shaolin Monk. Hundreds of students flooded his studio, and his life consisted of nothing but Kung Fu, night and day, seven days a week. At least until the day Leung Chao walked into his school.

She was the most beautiful lady he had ever seen, with a round face and high cheekbones, giving her a stately unique look. Her perfect almond-shaped, brown eyes and soft lips would be alluring to any man, even one who had taken a vow of celibacy. Best of all, she was an avid martial artist who had studied tai chi her entire life, but only a monk could take her skills to the next level, and Seng Shan was more than happy to oblige her. It didn't take long before master and student fell in love, and his monk vows were soon forgotten.

Shortly after their marriage, Chen was born, and they both devoted every ounce of their love to this amazing little girl. Not only did she excel in her Kung Fu skills, but academically she was always top of her class. Her parents were so proud of her accomplishments, and her future aspirations were unlimited.

Chen was in the back seat of Seng Shan's car, writing her speech for class valedictorian when the nukes hit Houston, but luckily her family was outside the city. They were on their way back from visiting several colleges she would never have the chance to attend.

"What do we do?" Chao asked as they stopped their car far from the city.

"The Kilgore's aren't far from here," Seng Shan answered as they turned the car around.

"Michael?" Chen asked from the back seat with raised eyebrows. "How can they help us?"

"I never told you," Seng Shan replied. "Thomas invited our family to stay with him if something like this happened."

"Who would have thought that eccentric doomsday prepper would be right," Chao stated.

"I'm confused. What am I missing?" Chen asked. "The only thing I know about the Kilgore's is they're wealthy, they're your students, and Michael is annoying."

"He's a nice boy," Chen's mother replied.

"If you say so," Chen said as she rolled her eyes. "You didn't answer my question. Do they have a fall-out shelter?"

"Yes, it's quite impressive," Seng Shan answered.

Impressive was an understatement. It was one of the most expensive shelters that money could buy, 2,400 square feet of living space buried twenty feet underground. It had four lavish bedrooms, two bathrooms, a gigantic generator room, and an 800-square-foot room filled with food supplies from the floor to the ceiling.

Mr. Kilgore's son Michael was the same age as Chen, and they had known each other ever since they were little. The boy was completely infatuated with Chen, following her around like a dog in heat. Unfortunately for the young man, Chen did not respond kindly to his advances. Nevertheless, twenty years of living underground with only one boy your own age can surely change your opinion, but poor Michael was hard-pressed for many years.

At first, Chen couldn't stand him, and they fought constantly. As a matter of fact, it was so bad during the first few years that Chen threatened to leave the shelter on several occasions. It took nearly fifteen years for things to turn in Michael's favor, and soon after, their child Fu was born.

Five more years passed, with the six of them crowded in the close confines, but in retrospect, it was some of Seng Shan's fondest memories. Young Fu didn't have the distractions of television or video games, like so many children before the Last War. His hours were devoted entirely to kung fu and academics. Actually, everyone was committed to this regime, as there wasn't really anything else to do. During the day, Chen would tutor them in every subject, and the afternoons would be full-blown Kung Fu training by Seng Shan.

The nightly entertainment consisted of cards or board games before they lay down to rest, but Monopoly, Life, and puzzles became quite monotonous after twenty years. Regardless of the unchanging routine, the close quarters truly brought them all together and created an inseparable, loving family.

The day finally arrived when they had no choice but to leave their protective shelter. With food supplies almost exhausted, they started sending out small foraging parties. Nuclear Winter had virtually killed off nearly all plant life and animals, especially those near major cities. The group was forced to travel to smaller towns and farms to find any sustenance. This mainly consisted of canned foods, and it was surprising to see how long some of these lasted beyond the expiration dates. When they couldn't find canned food, bugs became the delicacy. When hungry, it is amazing how quickly cockroaches can become a gourmet meal.

During one of these foraging trips the monk and his party came face to face with the first survivors of the holocaust. Not seeing any signs of life for more than a month, they became lackadaisical in their safety measures, splitting the party in two to cover more ground. While Seng Shan, his wife, and young Fu searched a gas station for supplies, the rest of the group went down the street to the grocery store.

They had just left the gas station when they heard the screams for help coming from down the street. With a clear view of the avenue, they could see at least a dozen people blocking the entrance to the grocery store. Seng Shan could hear his daughter frantically yelling, the sounds piercing his ears like daggers, but he couldn't see where she was with so many people blocking the store. Sprinting across the broken blacktop, the monk ran as fast as his old joints would allow, every step bringing him closer to the nightmare that would plague his dreams. Mr. Kilgore and Michael both lay motionless on the ground, and even from a distance, Seng Shan knew they were dead.

As he closed the gap, the monk drew his sword, and at the same time, he let out a deafening shout, which caused some of the people to turn his way. In that split second, he realized his adversaries weren't human, but he didn't have time to dwell on that thought. Like a tornado, his mighty sword cut through flesh and bone, arms and heads toppling to the ground. The creatures backpedaled, surprised at the formidable onslaught of the monk, and that's when Seng Shan saw his daughter slumped against the storefront door, her throat removed, jugular vein squirting blood in the air like a water fountain, as her lifeless eyes stared back at him.

"No!" he roared as an uncontrollable rage consumed him.

Body shaking, blood boiling, heart aching with misery, he killed every demon on that grim day. An hour passed before his blood lust subsided. Drenched from head to toe in crimson, he wasn't sure how many monsters he had killed. The ground was littered with flesh, chopped into so many parts that it was impossible to tell one demon from another.

Hands clenched, blood dripping from the nail marks he had dug into his palms, Seng Shan's traumatic memories were pushed aside, returning his thoughts to the present. Looking at his young disciples sleeping soundly on the floor, he thought, *many of you will die in the upcoming battle, but you won't regret it. Your hearts have suffered the same as mine, and I know you will give your lives for a chance at revenge.*

Quietly waking his people from their sleep, he commanded them to start stretching. One of them was given the duty to keep an eye on the sleeping guard. After they finished warming up, Seng Shan directed them through simulated parries and strikes with imaginary swords. They would continue these drills in the early hours of the morning until the guard awoke. Watching their progress, he said under his breath, "They're almost ready."

Katie

Right when the words left her lips, the demon lunged forward with eyes bulging, dropping the knife, the weapon clattering to the floor between it and Angelica. There had been a loud thumping noise from behind the demon, and Angelica realized the young girl must have struck the monster in the back of the head. Angelica saw her opportunity, and in one swift move, she picked up the knife and drove it upward, below the breastbone, into the creature's heart.

The monster's white eyes popped wide open in surprise as Angelica gazed into its face, the memory of her dead parents her only thought. The creature crumpled to the floor, revealing the young girl, who stood behind it with her makeshift weapon, pointing in the direction the demon once stood.

The girl had a crazed look in her dark brown eyes, mixed with a tinge of fear. Her skin was as dark as the misty clouds during the day, and her hair as black as they were at night. She was breathing heavily, and it took Angelica a few seconds to realize she was breathing just as hard as the young girl.

"I'm Angelica."

The girl tried to catch her breath and said in two mouthfuls, "I'm --- Katie."

"Katie, we need to leave. When they find the body, they'll kill you. You have to come with me," said Angelica, as she moved to the door to check if anyone was coming.

Not saying anything but nodding her approval, Katie followed Angelica to the door. Angelica peered out, eyes darting left and right. There weren't any demons close by, and the ones they could see were focusing their attention on the slaves rather than looking outside the village.

"Let's go," Angelica whispered.

Both girls bolted through the door, wrapping around the edge of the building and maneuvering between the empty structures. In no time whatsoever, they left the village behind them and were once again moving along the path toward Houston. Angelica had quickened her pace ever since they cleared the village, and Katie was doing her best to keep up, but she was getting tired.

"Can we slow down now? They can't see us anymore," asked Katie in between deep breaths.

"No, they may find the body and notice you're missing," Angelica answered with her hands on her knees and sweat dripping from her chin. "Also, I was following my friend when I stopped to help you. I need to catch up to him."

"What friend?" asked Katie.

"The man the demon army had bound as a prisoner. They stopped in your town earlier."

Katie ground to a halt and responded, "Are you crazy? You're trying to catch that army?"

Angelica stopped running, turned, and walked back to Katie, grabbed her by the shoulders, and calmly said, "My friend has been sent from God to stop the demons once and for all. He needs my help. You can come with me and fight for the side of the Lord, or you can go back to the slave camp. It's your decision, but I hope you come with me."

"I think you're nuts," replied Katie as she rolled her eyes. "But there's no way I'm going back to the camp."

"I'm not nuts, and if you stay with me, I'll prove it to you."

"Okay, lead the way," said Katie with uncertainty in her tone.

They continued jogging for about another half a mile until the army started to come into view. Now they could slow their pace and continue using what cover they could find to avoid detection. Their earlier rapid pace had made it nearly impossible for any communication, but now the communication flew freely enticed by curiosity, yet in whispers, as they didn't know how far their voices would travel.

"You know you're heading right into the demon's stronghold," said Katie.

"How do you know that?"

"Because I used to work there. It was only a month ago that they moved me out to the village we just left."

"What about your family? Were they back there in the town?"

"The demons killed them last year," answered Katie as she ground her teeth and clenched her fingers.

"I'm sorry... They murdered my parents two days ago."

"I'm sorry, too, and thank you for saving me back there," said Katie as her voice started to crack.

Angelica stepped forward and grabbed the girl, pulling her in tight. At first, Katie's arms remained at her side, but then the tears swelled in her eyes, and she ferociously returned the hug.

"I think we both saved each other," said Angelica as she separated and wiped the tears from her face.

Wiping her own tears, Katie smiled and said, "I think so."

The two girls continued following the demon army for several minutes until Angelica asked, "How many demons are there in Hus – town?"

Katie giggled, "It's pronounced Houston, and there are thousands. How are you going to help your friend against those odds?"

"I don't know, but the odds don't matter. If you had seen what I've seen, then you would know we have no other choice. My friend can destroy all of them. God's power flows through his veins."

"I don't know much about God, but if your warrior friend is so strong, then how was he captured?" asked Katie in a confident tone, thinking she had tricked Angelica.

"The army in front of us was more than four times that size when they attacked him. He killed hundreds of them before he was finally captured, and for the first time, I saw fear in the faces of the demons."

Then Angelica went into detail, explaining her own rescue and the events she witnessed at the battle.

"There is something special about this man, and if we can help him escape, then I believe he can save us all," Angelica stated.

Katie was deep in thought for a few seconds until she said, "I don't know if I believe everything you are telling me, but if there is a chance, then I'm willing to help. I know someone in Houston that we definitely have to talk to."

The Sickness?

It all happened so quickly, but what at first was pure elation in an instant turned to trepidation. We watched from the embankment as our dark friend killed demons by the hundreds, and I thought that for a moment, he would destroy the entire horde. Then one misfortune after another seemed to plague him due to the tactics of the human who was leading the demon army. First, his horse went down, then his swords were lost, and finally, the demons overwhelmed him.

Sadly, we watched as the army departed with our friend, and then we followed Angelica out to the battlefield. Blood and carnage were everywhere. It looked like a swamp of the dead, an entire acre coated in blood and body parts. Hands covered the ground like an army of giant spiders. Legs lay on the ground in another section, one set still standing straight up, propped up by other bodies. Pieces of flesh littered the floor, and hundreds of bodies were stacked in piles, creating macabre walls of the dead.

We shouted for Angelica to stop as she ran to our dark companion's horse, but she ignored our plea. We were afraid that the demons might still be alive but were relieved to see that everything on that battlefield was dead, except for the horse.

"We need to put it out of its misery," I said.

"I'll do it," Bill replied. He started walking toward the beast and the little girl, but before reaching them, Angelica lifted a blade high in the air and drove it into the animal.

"She's a lot tougher than I thought," I said.

"No kidding," Bill responded with raised eyebrows.

The army was almost lost to our view, so we informed Angelica that it was time to go. Frustratingly, she still wouldn't respond to us, but she must have heard our words because she started moving in that direction. Walking a few yards in front of us, the girl used what cover she could find to zigzag back and forth. She was a bright girl and must be worried that one of the demons would be watching for an attack from the rear. We tried to tell her what our years of experience had taught us. Demons never protected their backs. They were either too stupid, or they were too arrogant to believe anyone would attack them. But every time we tried to communicate with the girl, she would only ignore us.

"It's like she's a mini big guy," I said. "Sometimes I feel like we're invisible."

"R-E-S-P-E-C-T, JUST A LITTLE BIT, JUST A LITTLE BIT," Bill sang in his usual out-of-tune, irritating voice.

Bill was right. It seemed like both of us never received the respect we deserved. But in retrospect, Angelica and the big guy had both been through traumatic events. What these tragedies had done to their psyches was something Bill and I would never be able to comprehend. Because of this, we didn't try to push her any further. We simply let her lead the way, lost in her own thoughts.

Traveling this way for a while, losing sight of the army briefly and then establishing it once again, I noticed my stomach starting to cramp. It seemed to come and go. One minute I felt totally fine, and then the next second, I was racked by abdominal pain. I hadn't said anything about it until Bill broke the silence in his usual manner.

"My plumbing is playing tricks on me. I feel a poop storm coming on."

"I feel the same way. What did we eat?"

"The same thing we've been eating for days – boar burgers."

"Here it comes again!" I complained as I grabbed my stomach and hunched over.

"Me too!"

"I feel like I'm going to pass out!" I screamed as the sweat rolled down my cheeks.

"I feel the same. What the hell is going on?"

Both Bill and I were staring at each other in apparent agony, and then instantly, it was over. The pain disappeared, and I felt completely refreshed as if nothing had ever happened.

"How do you feel?" I asked Bill.

"I feel great."

"What just happened?" I asked. "Why is this happening to us at the same exact time?"

"Maybe we've been hanging out with each other for too long. If you start having orgasms the same time I do, then I'm leaving," Bill replied with lips spread from ear to ear.

That smile quickly turned to a painful look once again, as we were both racked with our dual sickness. This back and forth, agony to elation, continued several times as we followed Angelica. It seemed to finally subside when the remnants of a village appeared straight ahead. The closer we approached; we could see that the army had briefly come to a halt. But this only lasted a few minutes, and they were up again, moving toward the exit of the village.

We would have to detour around the town to avoid detection, but we would have to be fast or risk the chance of losing the army. We were about to relay this information to Angelica, but our smart girl had already figured it out and was making her way around the perimeter of the village. Using the cover of the abandoned structures, we sprinted on padded feet from one building to the next. Nearing the back of the town, we could still barely see the army on the horizon.

Then for no apparent reason, Angelica stopped and ran into the village. What was she doing? We couldn't yell to her, or the demons would know we were there. Standing there dumbfounded, seconds ticked by as we pondered our next course of action.

Then it happened again. The wrenching pain and dizziness entered my body. Glancing at Bill, I could see that he was in the same predicament. Turning my head, I scanned for Angelica, but she was lost from my sight. The sweat rolled down my face, and I violently started to heave. My body was shaking, and my head felt like it was a thousand degrees. Every fiber of my being felt like it was about to explode.

Looking to the South, I noticed the army was gone. All I could see was a trail of dust floating up into the air, left by their marching steps. Glancing at Bill, I saw he was experiencing the same agony as myself. Falling from our horses at the same time, we both landed on the ground twisting in discomfort, holding our stomachs in a fetal position.

Then I started to hallucinate. What else could explain what I was seeing? Before my eyes, Bill began to fade away. He looked at me, body twitching, eyes as big as baseballs, and I knew he could feel his evaporation. One second, he was there, and the next, he was gone. Quickly, I peered at my hands or where my hands should have been. And then I completely faded away.

Pain

I felt her lips upon me and the warmth of her tongue. Looking into her eyes, I felt our souls entwine. It was more than just passion. I loved her so deeply that one second away from her drilled a spike into my heart. How could I be so lucky?

She snuck a glance at me and laughed with that cute little chuckle that sounded so special. Breathing deeply, a combination of licorice and cinnamon attacked my senses, creating that unique scent that only belonged to her. I promised myself at that moment that I would never forget that laugh or the way she smelled.

You would think that after eighteen years together, our love would have lost its shine. On the contrary, I think it has grown even more through the years. As the time came nearer for us to head to the surface, it had actually brought us even closer together.

This made me return to the first time I had seen her. It was the day they launched the nukes, and we were evacuated to the government fallout shelter south of Dallas. With the end of the world confronting us, the last thing on my mind should be a pretty girl, but I couldn't help it. There were fifty of us herded into the underground chamber, and the Colonel started barking out orders as he gave us a tour of the facility.

To this day, I still can't remember a single word the man said, as I was blinded by the most gorgeous goddess of a woman I had ever seen. Her hair was jet black and curly, but it wasn't just a few curls; it was like a lightning bolt had plummeted to earth and created an explosive masterpiece of untamed sexiness. The hair draped down to the middle of her back, and I had an overwhelming urge to tangle my hands in it, becoming her lifelong prisoner. Her body was so thin that she couldn't tip the scales at more than one hundred pounds, yet I could see tight muscles in her exposed arms and knew the rest of her figure must be the same way.

I could only see her profile until this point, but she must have felt my stare because she turned toward me and smiled for a brief second before looking back at the Colonel. If my jaw wasn't attached to my face, I'm sure it would have dropped to the floor. That glimpse at her beautiful brown eyes, surrounded by a perfect tan complexion, and the cute little mole on her right cheek cast a mesmerizing spell over me from that day forward.

I was such an idiot that it took me nearly a month to build up the courage to talk to her. It was pure luck that no one else came in and swept her away. It wasn't until years later that she told me she had been waiting for me ever since that first day I had seen her. But then I finally gathered my nerves and talked to her, and after that, everything moved at warp speed.

It was only a week later that the Colonel married us, and only ten months after that, our daughter was born. I still remember that day so clearly. Holding my little girl for the first time and feeling her soft baby skin against my arms, I dropped to my knees that night and thanked God for making me the happiest man alive.

My recollections skipped back to the present, and my wife and I turned simultaneously to look at our daughter. She was shouting orders to other survivors from our community. They were packing up supplies and getting ready to finally head to the surface. She turned and gave us a thumbs-up signal and a big smile. She had become such a wonderful young lady, turning into an inspirational leader who everyone respected. We were so proud of her.

I glanced back into my wife's eyes and saw the glow that we both shared for Angelica --- wait, --- that isn't her name. Why can't I remember my daughter's name?

My look digs deeper into my wife's eyes, and I see my own reflection. I see fear on my face, --- and pain. My wife turns to liquid and melts away from my hands. Quickly, I turn, dig my toes into the ground, and try to explode toward my daughter. Every step is like quicksand, and no matter how hard I try, I can't get any closer. She opens the shelter door, a look of shock forming across her face, and she starts to scream. The pain absorbs me. It cuts into my bones and tears my soul away. A path opens to my right, drenched in darkness, beckoning me to enter, promising me my pain will be gone forever. I also know that if I take it, my memories of my family will be lost forever. Gritting my teeth, I try to fight, but I can't endure the pain. I'm too weak. I've failed them. I choose the dark path...

My body wakes drenched in sweat. For a moment, a dream lingers in my mind, but instantly the images are lost. An urge gnaws at me to remember, but no matter how hard I focus, it will not return.

The real-world returns and I realize my body is in pain. Why do so many people fear pain? During my travels with Bill and the other guy, I had seen people complain about it and run from it. For me, pain had always been my friend. It gave me purpose. It awakened my senses to let me know my mistakes. If I was cut, then I hadn't moved fast enough. If my muscles were sore, then I had neglected to prepare them for battle. So, when I awoke with a throbbing pain in the back of my head and felt the flesh scraped from my back, I didn't complain. Instead, I invited my friend in to teach me what I had done wrong.

My mistake had been losing control. My emotions had got the best of me, and by doing this, decreased my chance of escape.

Lying on my back, my feet and hands are bound as Abraham's horse drags me across the ground. The small rocks and sand tear into my back as I am pulled along with a lack of courtesy.

I try to lift my head and feel a wave of dizziness. My memories slowly come back, and I realize the demons must have hit me on the back of my head. How long had I been out? Then I remembered Angelica running toward the village, and my heartbeat quickened. Is she safe?

Lifting my head, I shake away the dizziness. I try to look between the legs of the demons that surround me. My muscles clench, and I feel the dark rage begin to rise inside of me. Then I catch a glimpse of them. They are still following me, but another young girl is with them. Who is she?

The Lord's Prayer

I could hear my horse breathing and the slow rhythm of his footsteps. My eyes opened to crystal clarity, and the path before me was revealed. Angelica was walking a few yards ahead, but another girl was at her side. This girl was slightly taller than Angelica, and her hair was dark black, pulled into a long ponytail. She was wearing an old, tattered t-shirt, stained in several spots, and ripped blue jeans. Her thin arms were exposed, revealing dark brown skin.

Glancing to my left, I caught Bill looking at me. He raised his shoulders, giving me the signal that he was as clueless as I was. Confused, I looked to the horizon and realized an incredible amount of time had passed. The army was in the distance, but I could also see the remnants of thousands of structures spread out from east to west. However, what truly caught my eye was one gigantic tower standing in the distance. It was the biggest thing I had ever seen.

"What is that?" I asked.

"Wow, that thing is big. I'm having a huge case of penis envy," Bill responded.

"Can you be serious for a minute? What's going on? How did we get here, and who is that little girl?"

"I know as much as you do. The last thing I remember is passing out."

"We didn't pass out. We disappeared."

"No way, you're going bonkers!"

"It's the truth, and you know it. I saw it in your eyes just before you vanished."

Bill stopped his horse, took a breath, and started chewing on his lower lip. "Maybe we time traveled."

"I think it's more than that. The big guy told us to stay with the girl, and we didn't listen. When she ran to that building, we didn't follow her. Maybe our dark friend has powers we don't understand, and he was punishing us."

"That's a load of crap."

Bill may have said he didn't believe my theory, but I noticed he quickly moved closer to Angelica. Realizing this might be a prudent move, I also spurred my steed forward. I now had a clear view of our new member and could tell she was of Hispanic descent, with dark hair, dark skin, and beautiful brown eyes. From her height, I estimated she was approximately eleven years old. The girl carried herself with a powerful look of determination, reminding me a lot of Angelica. Her clothes were in disarray; broken sandals and a torn pair of blue jeans accompanied by a t-shirt with the word A-S-T-R-O-S on it. I had no idea what that word meant.

Hoping for more information, I was just about to ask our new companion her name when both girls ducked behind a small pile of scattered bricks and steel. Bill and I decided to dismount and also seek cover. We were very close to Hus-town and decided it would be best to leave the horses behind and go the rest of the way on foot.

It wasn't difficult to find places to hide, as the remains of broken buildings were everywhere you looked. The girls sprinted from one structure to the next, always staying in the shadows. They were moving so fast that Bill and I were hard-pressed to keep up with them.

Keeping the army in sight, we were one block over from

path 45, following a narrow corridor, between a long line of structures. The passage was only about four feet wide, and most of the way was clear of obstructions. Occasionally broken rubble and bricks blocked the way, and we were forced to climb over the impediments. This slowed our pace but didn't prevent us from making fantastic time, and we had almost caught up to the army when tragedy arose.

The girls were in the lead, and we had just climbed over a hill of broken concrete. There was a back door to our right, and as we passed, it opened, and a demon appeared. The creature let out a piercing scream and ran toward us. We took off running, feet scrunching on the loose stones and pebbles, arms pumping as quickly as possible, but the monster continued its howls, pursuing us and alerting anyone nearby of our presence.

As bad luck would have it, we heard answering yells coming from the demon army one block to our right. Passing an opening, we could see the army racing toward us, hooting, and howling with excitement. Darting my eyes to the left, I noticed a crossing corridor approaching, but it was blocked by two buildings that had collapsed into each other. Glancing back to the right as we flew by, I saw dozens of demons sprinting down the street in hot pursuit.

"The next cross-section is a quarter mile down the corridor!" I screamed in between deep breaths, but the girls didn't appear to hear my words.

The demons were gaining ground, their long strides flying across the pavement. The girls were in front of us, furiously pumping their little legs, sweat glistening on their arms, wet spots soaking through their shirts.

Fear drove us on, driving imaginary spurs into our legs as we ran as we had never run before. Caution was thrown aside, as every step put us at risk of failure. The girls jumped over bricks and loose debris. They leaped over potholes and cracks in the pavement, and each time I held my breath, thinking they would break an ankle. Some of the demons behind us tripped and fell, screaming in agony or frustration. But it wasn't enough, as another creature was always there to take its place.

We were getting close to the cross-section, but it wouldn't matter. They were almost upon us, and there was nothing we could do to stop them. Angelica was a few feet ahead of me, and I saw her turn her head to glance behind us. She must have known there was no escape, so she shouted to our new companion, "Katie, I'll slow them down! Go find him!"

Then Angelica stopped, spun around, and faced the demon army. I thought to myself, what could this brave little girl do that would give Katie a chance to escape? We also turned to face the demon horde, knowing that they would plow through us and grab Katie in an instant. Angelica dropped to her knees, put her hands together, looked toward the sky, and shouted.

"Our Father, which art in heaven, Hallowed be thy Name. Thy Kingdom come. Thy will be done in earth, as it is in heaven. Give us this day our daily bread. And forgive us our trespasses, as we forgive those that trespass against us. And lead us not into temptation, but deliver us from evil."

As soon as Angelica began to speak, the demons slid to a halt, many of them dropping to the floor as they started screaming in agony. They slapped their hands against their heads, covering their ears, and rolled on the ground like their skin was on fire. Their bodies shook and gyrated as if the words coming from Angelica were poison arrows plunging into their dark hearts. Their agony immediately ceased as soon as Angelica stopped praying, and then they were upon us. The monsters threw Angelica to the ground so hard that I thought for sure they would tear her to pieces. This probably would have been the case if it wasn't for their leader. He moved his horse into the middle of the conflict, knocking demons to the side and shouting commands.

"Don't hurt her!" the human leader yelled as he trotted up

to Angelica.

The demons obeyed immediately and roughly yanked Angelica to her feet. She stood there bruised and battered, blood running from her nose, and her shirt was torn in several spots. However, her appearance didn't break her spirit, as her chin remained high in a regal manner with defiance in her eyes.

"What is your name, girl?" the leader demanded.

"Angelica," she responded.

"Angelica the Angel," he chuckled mockingly. "The Lord's Prayer may work on demons, but it won't work on me. The Master will be very pleased to meet you. He will break you and show you a new Lord to follow."

The leader commanded his demons to bind our hands and tie us to his horse. It definitely wasn't the situation we wanted to be in, but at least we were reunited with our dark companion. But he didn't seem to share our enthusiasm. If he had laser vision, then the look he gave us surely would have melted us to dust.

"Why did you follow me?" he demanded in a whisper once the army started to move.

I was about to respond when Angelica interjected, "I couldn't leave you."

"I told you to stay with them," replied our dark friend as he nodded in our direction.

Angelica glanced at us and then looked back at him with scrunched eyebrows. "I don't know what you're talking about, but don't worry, my friend Katie went to get help."

Katie's Mission

Katie rocketed down the alley, her feet barely touching the ground. Angelica's sacrifice won't be in vain! She would put as much distance as she safely could between her and the demon army, but she had to be careful. The city was thriving with demons, and if she was going to accomplish her mission, she couldn't be captured.

Luckily, she had grown up in the city and knew it fairly well. After a couple of miles, she slowed her pace and continued moving through the alleyways, careful to stay in the shadows. She could tell that Angelica had prevented any pursuit, but at what cost? *Is she still alive?* Her belief in God was dangerous, and if the demons found out, they would surely kill her.

Katie's parents never taught her about God, but she had heard rumors from other people. Some said that God existed once, but he had died. Others said that people had stopped believing in him, so God had left. From what Katie had learned about God being all-powerful, she doubted that he could be killed, but he probably did leave, and humans probably deserved it.

Katie had seen many horrible things in her short life, and they weren't all done by demons. She had seen husbands betray wives and brothers betray sisters. One time she saw a woman give her own baby to the demons for sacrifice. The woman was given a choice to take her own life rather than give up the child, but she obviously loved herself more.

Katie had met many evil people, but she had also met many people with genuinely pure hearts. One of these was Angelica. She had barely met her, but it was hard to deny the radiance of good she exuded. It was a strange feeling that at first, she didn't know how to put it into words. It almost seemed like Angelica had an invisible bubble of good surrounding her. The closer you got to her, the stronger the feeling. She didn't know what God was, but when she tried to picture him in her mind, all she could think of was that feeling Angelica gave her. Maybe God had forgotten about humans, but he hadn't forgotten Angelica.

This thought and her hatred for demons pushed her resolve forward. She would do everything she could to save Angelica and her warrior friend. If they were already dead, she would avenge them and all the others she had seen killed through the years. However, to do this, she had to reach the man she knew from Houston. *He's the only one who can help us.*

With cat-like steps, she moved through the alleyways for another hour, using the debris to hide her from any prying eyes. The closer she came to the center of the city, the debris diminished, and her chances of being caught increased. *It's time to execute stage two of my plan.* She needed to get across town, and the only way to do that without being seen was through the sewers.

The girl had never entered the sewers before, but she had heard the stories. Very few people returned after venturing into their depths, and those who had come back spoke tales of giant monsters that devoured people whole. She didn't know if these stories were true, but what other option did she have? She would have to take the gamble.

Katie could see the alleyway was ending, and an intersection loomed ahead. Like an assassin, she crept up to the edge of the wall and slithered one eye into the open, searching for demons. The coast was clear, and a sewer cover was about fifty feet away along the sidewalk. Quickly, she dashed to the cover, reached down, stuck her fingers in the hole, and pulled. The heavy steel wouldn't budge.

Running back to the alleyway, Katie started rummaging through the rubble. She needed some kind of lever. Wide-eyed, she searched for several minutes, diving into bricks and concrete until her hands bled. She had just about given up hope when finally, a piece of dark metal appeared beneath some bricks. A smile crossed her face, and she started flinging obstructions left and right. The metal kept getting longer until a piece of steel rebar about four feet in length was exposed. She yanked the bar from the rubble and headed back to the sewer cover.

Katie shoved the bar into one of the holes and tried to push down, but nothing happened. She moved all the way to the end of the bar and pushed down with all her might, muscles shaking, sweat growing on her brow. The cover didn't even budge, so she hung over the bar, lifting herself off the ground and putting her full weight on it. The metal cover moved, but barely an inch. *Maybe a grown man could move this cover, but there's no way my little body has the strength to do it. How could I be so stupid?* All this time, her great plan had depended on getting into the sewers, yet she had never considered how heavy the covers were. *I'll have to find another way.*

Running a few feet down the street, she inspected the water drain along the edge of the sidewalk. *Everyone says how skinny I am. Maybe I can fit.* Katie got down on her belly and peered inside. It was pitch black, and she couldn't see the bottom. *What's down there? Will some huge monster bite my head off if I stick it inside?* She had to take the chance. Creeping closer, her hands pushing small pebbles of broken blacktop into the opening, she pushed her head against the cold cement. It started to slide through, but then she felt the tension, so she started to wiggle her head back and forth. The pain on her temples increased, squeezing and gnawing at her flesh, removing hair and skin. She wiggled a little more, and pop her head burst through like a newborn being delivered.

"Yes," she shouted gleefully under her breath.

Reaching into her pocket, Katie pulled out the lighter that her mother had given her on her tenth birthday. It was only a few days later that her parents were killed, but she couldn't think about that painful memory now. She remembered how her mother had told her to use it only during an emergency, and this certainly qualified. Wiggling her arm through the hole, she turned on the lighter. It didn't provide much light, but it was enough to make out the walls and floor of the sewer. She could faintly see and hear the water flowing at the bottom, approximately five feet beneath her. There was no way she could continue to enter headfirst, as the fall would probably cause her harm.

Turning the lighter off, Katie swiftly returned it to her pocket. The girl started to wiggle backward on her stomach, slowly pulling her head out of the drain. The pain throbbed in her temples as her head scraped against the concrete and tore off even more skin. Removing her head entirely from the drain, she checked the cut to see how bad it was. It was dripping blood, but luckily it wasn't too serious.

Scooting completely around, she started lowering her body feet first through the opening. This caused her to tremble, as she couldn't see where she was going. Katie began to imagine creatures grabbing at her legs and dragging her down into the darkness. Trying to move faster, she pushed her body all the way through until only her head remained.

Feeling the tension like she had previously, she started to squirm her head back and forth, but for some reason, this time, she couldn't get through. She was stuck and started to panic as she thought she heard footsteps moving through the sewer. A giant monster could be coming to eat her, and there was nothing she could do to stop it. Kicking violently from side to side, she started to yank her head back and forth, all the while pushing with her hands. The pain was excruciating, and she could feel the blood dribbling down her cheek. The coppery taste entered her mouth as sweat dripped into her eyes, blinding her vision. *I must free myself. This can't be the way I die with my friend so desperately counting on me.* Her body shook, and she felt like screaming, but what good would that do. Nobody was coming to help.

Then she thought about Angelica, and she stopped moving, slowing down her breath and calming her mind. Angelica's faith in God gave her hope. Maybe he could help her.

"I know that I've never believed in you, but I could sure use your help now. My friends need me, and if you help me out today, I promise to devote my life to you."

Taking a deep breath, Katie put her hands and feet against the sewer wall and pushed with all her might. Her head started to move, but it hurt worse than before. Ignoring the pain, she pushed with every fiber of energy her little body could muster. Inch by inch, she slithered her head through, and then abruptly, like a baby being born, she popped through and fell into the water. The girl sat there motionless, breathing heavily for several seconds.

"Thank you, God. I will never forget what you did for me."

Looking up at the sewer drain, Katie could see the soft light peeking through the opening. It barely illuminated the area. Scanning her eyes in both directions, she could only see a few feet down the tunnel. Then she thought about the lighter and fearfully went to her pocket. There were only a few inches of water underneath her, but if the lighter had gotten wet, it would be ruined. She pulled it from her pocket and quickly ascertained that it was still dry. Breathing a sigh of relief, she rolled her thumb along the flint wheel, igniting the flame. It only lit the area a few feet in front of her, but it would have to do.

Standing up, she brushed the muck from her pants, cracked her neck, and started to move down the tunnel. She had a mission to complete and refused to let anything stop her from accomplishing it.

Fear

We continued trudging along toward the tower, each step growing heavier by the minute. Looking down at my shoes, I remembered that long ago they had been white, but the years had been cruel and changed them to a rusty brown. The dust had slowly eaten them away and darkened what was once so clean, their frayed laces flopping in the wind, just like my hopes.

Our dark friend was dragged along the ground, sometimes over dirt and sometimes over the exposed pavement. Seeing the sharp rocks or broken glass lying in his path, I badly wanted to shout out a warning, but there was nothing I could do. His back would slide over them, leaving a trail of blood, yet his face remained indifferent to the pain.

Glancing to my left, I saw Bill marching at my side, and I could see the look of concern on his face. Then I looked to my right and saw a tear roll down Angelica's cheek. I don't think we are getting out of this alive. We will be brought before this Master and tortured to death. Fear crept into my bones. My own fear of the pain I would suffer, and most of all, the fear for my friends.

What is fear? I have pondered this question many times over the last five years. Why do some people have more fear than others? My dark friend doesn't know the meaning of the word, yet Bill and I have experienced it many times. --- However, maybe he does know fear. Surely not his own fear of dying, but perhaps he fears for the life of his companions. Since he has hardly ever spoken, it is hard to know if he really cares what happens to Bill or me, but Angelica is a different story. I know he cares about her by the way he looks at her.

There is a longing in his eyes that she has woken. Something inside of him has returned that I thought was lost. He's starting to change. When I look into those blue eyes, I see something --- human. Before his eyes almost seemed like a demon's eyes. They were dead, lifeless, and without emotion. Now I see a flicker of moisture, where before, they were dry and unforgiving.

Is that the answer? Can someone without fear not be able to cry? It is said that of all the animals on the planet, humans are the only ones who can create tears. Isn't this a weakness of our species? Don't we teach our young boys not to cry? We tell them, "Toughen up, stop being such a cry baby." We push them to keep their feelings hidden, otherwise, we assume someone will take advantage of them. How does the saying go? --- Nice guys finish last.

The stereotype of a man who shows his emotions is someone who will not be successful, someone who is unattractive and can't provide for his family. This stereotype has pushed men to become something without compassion. It has desensitized him from the needs of others. No wonder the Final War occurred, and man destroyed our planet. No wonder God abandoned us and let evil preside over what is left.

Nevertheless, I see a ray of hope. If someone who was as lost as my dark companion can start to change, then maybe all humankind can change. This world is blanketed in fear now, but maybe we need fear to wake up our emotions. Maybe crying isn't a weakness but a way for fear to leave our bodies and give us the courage to fight.

We reach the tower...

The Sewers

It was like a mouth of impenetrable blackness as the young girl entered the damp, cold snake that wound its way under the worms and other bugs that crawled above. The echoes of footsteps were the only thing to relieve the loneliness inside the giant serpent as their sound rebounded off the walls. Shadows dissolved as quickly as they appeared, giving her nothing but darkness to look forward to.

The gloom of the unknown penetrated the tunnels as it penetrated Katie's mind. Step by step, her feet splashed through the water and excrement of the bowels of the city. Her only comfort in the darkness was her lighter, which barely benefited her vision. Nevertheless, humans have a remarkable ability to adapt, and her eyes began to grow accustomed to the black tunnels. She could now see several feet in front of her and occasionally even further when she came across another sewer drain.

On these occasions, she pulled herself up and peered through the drain to check her location. Down in the dark, it was easy to lose your way, and she wanted to make sure she was still headed in the right direction. Hundreds of demons and slaves were on the streets, moving about in their daily activities.

The demons were forcing the slaves to rebuild the city. They cracked their whips, punishing and prodding the slaves into obedience. *What other choice do they have?* The freedom of choice no longer existed. The only freedom that remained was death, and in her short life, Katie had seen this freedom carried out many times. Suicide was the one choice the demons could not control, and several people she knew had preferred this means of escape.

As Katie continued sloshing through the dark sewers, her thoughts turned to the past, and the tunnels she traversed bore into her soul. They opened the wet sore that would not heal, festering and growing into something she had tried to forget. Maybe it was the lack of light that let these cold memories return, or could it be the solitude and monotony that cracked her heart and bled emotion.

Katie returned to that day and felt a shiver run through her body. She wanted to block the memory, but no matter how hard she tried, it returned with a vengeance. She could see her parents' faces so clearly. Her father's strong chin and bright eyes comforted her from the loneliness of the tunnels. Her mother's smile lit up the way more than any lighter could ever hope to accomplish.

She remembered them huddled together on that fateful morning. During the night, the demons would shackle them together to prevent any slaves from escaping. The nights were her favorite, for it was the only time she could huddle close to her parents and feel their love. They planted gentle kisses on her forehead and whispered "I love you" in her ears. Fading away into her dreams, she would leave the horrible abuses of the day behind. She dreamed of running free and playing with her friends. She dreamed of laughter and love.

The crack of a whip startled her, and her dreams of happiness were shattered. She awoke to hear the shouts of demons as they stirred the slaves to start another day of misery. Katie and her parents got up, wiped the sleep from their eyes, and moved as quickly as they could. The shackles connecting the three of them made this difficult, but they managed to shuffle into line with the rest of the slaves.

There were about thirty slaves in this camp, and their current project was to repair a factory. This factory would be used to make horse-drawn wagons. Wagons and sailboats were a major necessity as they had now become the quickest way of transportation, sending crops and weapons to the demon armies.

Katie's dad and several other men were repairing the back wall of the building. Part of it had caved in, and Katie's dad was relaying the concrete block. Katie and her mom were about fifty feet away, mixing the mortar required to fix the wall.

They had been working on this project for two weeks, and during this time, one of the demons became problematic. The creature continued to harass Katie's mother, and its advances became bolder every day. At first, it started with light slaps to her backside when it passed, but yesterday the monster grabbed her breast with one hand and shoved the other into her crotch. The creature whispered its vile intentions into her ear, all the while staring straight at Katie's father. Katie's dad glanced back for a brief second, but then he quickly dropped his eyes. The demon laughed, walking away with a swagger of superiority in its stride.

Yesterday was lost to history, and Katie's family didn't see the demon again, but the new morning spurred sorrow that Katie would never forget. They were all working in the same positions as the previous day when the demon once again headed toward Katie's mother. Katie kept her eyes glued on the monster, noticing a different demeanor in the grotesque creature. As it came toward them, it continued to grab its crotch, licking and biting its lips.

Katie nudged her mother and said, "It's coming."

"Don't do anything," her mother warned. "It can take my body, but it will never take my soul."

The creature didn't say a word. It simply walked up, grabbed Katie's mom, and threw her to the floor in front of everyone. Next, it ripped off her mother's underwear and mounted her. Her body shaking, Katie shot glances at the other slaves, but they all averted their stares. Tears poured out of the young girl's eyes as she shuffled her feet and pulled on her hair. She looked at her mom, seeing the painful look on her face as the demon continued to thrust his body back and forth on top of her. Katie stepped forward, but her mother put up her hand, signaling her not to interfere.

Katie was still looking at her mother when her mom's eyes bulged, and the skin on her forehead rose at it pulled her eyebrows upward. Her stare was focused behind Katie, but before she could turn and follow her gaze, a blur rushed past her. Katie's father flew in, tackling the demon to the ground, rolling over and over, punching and biting.

Katie's mother rose to her feet, rushed to her husband, and tried to pull the man off, but before she could help him, other demons had arrived. They grabbed Katie's dad and threw him against the wall, restraining the man.

The demon that had raped Katie's mom scrambled to its feet, blood dripping from its nose. It walked over to Katie's father with unsteady steps and stared at him with blazing eyes. The creature turned back toward the slaves with its arms shaking and the muscles in its face twitching.

Looking directly at Katie, it said, "This is what happens when you disobey us."

Without a second thought, the demon pulled out a knife, pressed it against the neck of Katie's father, and slit his throat.

Katie's mother screamed and bolted toward the demon. The monster still held the knife in its hand, so she lunged forward and grabbed its arm with both hands. The creature tried to yank the appendage back, but it was too late. Katie's mom pulled her head down, and in one swift motion, cut her own throat.

The drip, drip of the faucet was all you could hear in that lonely tunnel, but it wasn't a faucet that was leaking. Katie had stopped moving. She stood frozen in that dark tunnel, except for the tears that rolled down her face and plunged into the sewer water. She missed her parents so much, but she also hated them, especially her mother. *How could she abandon me to a world filled with evil?*

"How could you do that?" she shouted down the tunnel, but the only answer that echoed back was her own question.

She already knew the answer but didn't like to admit it. Her mother wasn't as strong as Katie was, and she had taken the easy way out. But it was difficult to blame her. Most of the slaves were weak and lacked the courage to fight back. --- But she wasn't like her mother.

Wiping the tears away, Katie returned her focus to the sewers. Ears wide open, she thought she heard splashes in the tunnel behind her. Quickly turning her head, she peered in that direction, but nothing alerted her senses to danger. Maybe the ominous sound had just been her imagination. Feet sloshing through the muck, she started down the tunnel, but that eerie feeling that someone was following her loomed in her mind.

The water splashed with each step as she moved closer to her goal, each footfall echoing ahead and behind like some phantom cry. Checking another sewer drain, she realized her destination was only a mile away. Her excitement caused her to pick up the pace, and that's when she heard the splashes behind her grow louder. *That wasn't my imagination*. Something was following her, and she could clearly hear gigantic limbs sloshing through the sewage. Letting out a gasp, the girl started to run, but the quicker she moved, the louder the noises behind her increased. Whatever was chasing her knew she was trying to escape.

Vigorously pumping her legs, she ran as fast as she could, but unfortunately, the water and muck slowed her down, sticking to her shoes like glue. A long screeching growl echoed off the tunnel walls, and she realized the creature chasing her was very close and very big. Sweat slithered down her body as chills climbed up her spine. A sewer drain emerged ahead on the right. Regardless of the risk of detection, she decided it was time to leave the dark tunnels behind her.

Reaching the drain, Katie jumped up and grabbed the ledge. Pulling herself up, she tried to poke her head through, but the opening was too tight. *Crap, some of the sewer drains must be smaller than others. What if all the drains are smaller? What if there is no way out of here?*

Katie started to run again. She could no longer hear her own feet splashing as the splashes from behind grew in intensity. Ahead, she could see that the tunnel turned sharply to the left. When she came to the turn, she briefly glanced back down the tunnel as she continued to run. Her heart froze, prodding her feet to heedless speed. She had heard stories of giant alligators in the sewers, but she never imagined they could be this big.

The monster barely fit in the sewer. It had to be almost five feet high from the bottom of its feet to the top of its head. Katie couldn't see how long it was, but she guessed it had to be nearly thirty feet. The creature must have seen her, for it launched itself forward at unrestrained speed, its enormous tail swooshing back and forth, smacking the concrete walls and sending explosive vibrations through the corridor.

As the young girl ran, her heart pounded in her throat, sweat exploding from every pore, and to make matters worse, she was starting to feel dizzy. It had been a long time since she had eaten, and she had been pushing her body beyond its means. *How much longer can I last?* The alligator was getting closer, and the tunnel started to decline deeper. There weren't any sewer drains ahead or any means of escape that she could see. All seemed lost…

Duel With The Devil

For as far as you could see, the ground around it was blanketed with ash and charcoal. Sometimes the wind would swoop in with all its hatred and churn mini dust devils of death. To look upon it gave you a feeling of raw sorrow. What once gave life to so many souls was now nothing more than a graveyard without markers. The only tombstone was the tower, standing alone, reaching its claws up into the dark clouds a thousand feet away.

It seemed endless, disappearing into the dark mists, hiding its true height. I should have felt amazed, but somehow, I felt this wasn't the first time I had looked upon a building this high. However, I couldn't help but be impressed by the beauty of this formidable structure. The alluring sparkle from the acres of glass was almost blinding. It seemed totally untouched by the Last War and seemingly out of place. How could it remain unfazed? Everywhere around it was destruction, yet somehow the tower remained untouched. It had to be magical.

Dismissing most of his army, Abraham left only a dozen demons to accompany us into the tower. We entered the main doors on the west side of the building, and immediately I was taken aback. I thought the outside was impressive, but it paled in comparison to the inside lobby. Everything was immaculate. The tile floors shined so brightly that at first, I thought they were freshly mopped. Gold covered the walls and furniture, but actually, I'm not sure if it was real gold. It didn't really matter, considering gold no longer held any value, but it still looked impressive. Gorgeous paintings were hanging on every wall, and one gigantic picture covered an entire area from floor to ceiling. It must have been fifty feet high and one-hundred feet long.

Our dark friend couldn't be trusted to walk, so his legs remained bound. A couple of the demons dragged him across the floor with the rope from Abraham's horse. Angelica, Bill, and I were free to use our legs, but our hands remained tied, and Angelica's mouth was gagged with a small rag. We moved past several doors until we finally came to one that was marked "stairs."

From here, we started our ascent, moving upward floor by floor, step by agonizing step, climbing a stairway into the heavens but probably leading us on a path to hell. The demons were forced to carry our dark companion, rotating partners every twenty floors. We kept our eyes open, looking for some means to escape, but all we could see was hopelessness. Nothing could be more troublesome than the final trek to torture. What else could we possibly face when we reached the Master? Looking at Angelica, I observed her soft, innocent features and only hoped they would kill her quickly. If not, then I hoped they would kill me first. I dreaded having to watch her suffer.

After what seemed like an eternity, we finally reached the end of our journey. The door loomed in front of me, and I realized it was probably the last one we would ever enter. Whatever evil faced us on the other side would surely be beyond imagination. This Master must be a demon nightmare, that to just look upon him would drive fear through the staunchest warrior.

Abraham opened the door, and we were ushered into the room. It was a gigantic space, and standing in the middle was the most beautiful man I had ever seen. The man was dressed in a simple white robe, but it appeared so clean it was beyond description. He had long flowing blond hair that reached past his shoulders. It looked so smooth that all I could think of was running my hands through it. His face was perfect, with a strong chin and striking blue eyes. As I looked at those eyes, I felt a call to dive in and swim my worries away. They promised relaxation and enjoyment. Images of naked women floated into my thoughts, and they wanted me. They touched me. They made me climax over and over in endless euphoria. Then the man smiled and walked toward us with his arms wide open, inviting us into his embrace. I wanted to run toward him and feel those strong arms comfort me, but instead, he hugged my dark friend.

The man opened his mouth, and the sounds that came forth were magical. "I am so glad to finally meet you. I've been waiting for this moment for such a long time. I've been watching you, and I must say I have never been so impressed. Your skill is remarkable!"

Looking at my friend, I expected him to say thank you to this wonderful man, but instead, all I saw was turmoil on his face. He seemed to struggle with his emotions as the muscles on his face twitched back and forth.

My jaw dropped when he mumbled, "I'm going to kill you."

Why would he say that to this incredible man? The man started laughing and responded, "Why would you want to kill me? What have I done to deserve your contempt?"

The man turned to Abraham and asked, "Did you mistreat him or his friends?"

"No, --- no Master, they were both brought to you unmolested,"

"Both?" the Master asked with raised eyebrows and a tilt to his head.

Abraham looked perplexed and didn't know what to say. He was about to speak when the man cut him off and said with a chuckle, "Abraham, your eyes are open, but you are not able to see what I see. This warrior is a confused man, a man that carries much guilt."

The man turned back to our dark companion and said, "You do not need to carry this guilt any longer. I can free you from it."

As the man finished his sentence, Angelica began to squirm and mumble through the rag in her mouth. The man turned to her and said, "Who is this beautiful, sweet child? Why have you covered her mouth, Abraham? Remove it immediately!"

I could see that Abraham was perturbed, but he did as he was bid. Then the man knelt in front of Angelica, looked her in the eye, and said, "Such a pretty girl. Don't worry, I won't hurt your friend."

Angelica screamed, "Get away from me, you vile demon! I see you for what you really are!"

The man jumped to his feet, eyes bulging and a slight tremor in his frame. He took a few unsteady steps backward, and for a split second, I saw through Angelica's eyes. I saw darkness and disgust. I saw pure evil. It was just a glimpse, and then he returned to his normal form, but the brightness was gone, and I knew he was only a façade.

The Master was aghast and shouted at Abraham, "Gag her mouth and remove her from the room!"

"Why not kill her, my Lord?" Abraham asked with concern.

The Master seemed to contemplate this for a second but then responded, "No! Make sure no harm befalls her. When the time is right, she will be a great sacrifice to our Lord."

"Yes, Master."

Our dark friend watched as one of the demons removed Angelica from the room. Their gaze met, and I could see the compassion in their eyes. When she was gone, our companion turned, and it seemed as if a new face had grown where the old one once resided. Compassion was hidden away, and the warrior was released.

"You repulsive monster!" he screamed as the spittle sprayed from his mouth. "Untie me, and I'll rip your head off! --- Face me, you coward!"

The Master's eyebrows bounced up and down, and a huge grin crossed his face.

"Yes! --- Let your rage out. Don't hold it in. So, you want to taste my blood? --- Why should I deny you what you hunger for? --- Abraham, cut his bonds, and give this man his swords."

Abraham did as was commanded, but he cautiously moved back several yards, before sliding the weapons to my warrior friend. In the meantime, the Master went to the far wall and removed two pristine Samurai swords hanging there as part of the room's décor. I was surprised that the demons and Abraham would allow their Master to fight such a formidable adversary. But my doubts about their strategical experience were soon put to rest when I saw the Master move. I should have known when Angelica showed me a glimpse of what he truly was. This man didn't move like a human.

They charged in, and steel met steel. The song of swords began as metal clanked against metal, sending vibrations throughout the room. For someone who had just entered the suite and didn't know what was happening, they might have laughed. It almost seemed comical as the two warriors seemed to be only waving their arms at each other from a few feet away. It only appeared this way because both of their weapons couldn't be seen. They moved with such incredible speed that I couldn't fathom how either of them blocked each of their attacks. Yet block they did, and after several minutes they separated with neither of them landing a mark.

They circled each other, breathing heavily. Both of their chests rising and falling, thirsting for oxygen to fuel their muscles. The Master wore a massive grin on his face, chuckling as he paced the floor. If my warrior friend could fire arrows from his eyes, then the Master would surely be dead. His stare was hatred unleashed, but I thought for a second, I saw a small piece of doubt on his countenance.

The Master must have seen it also, for he said, "You know you can't beat me. --- Join me, and I will make you, my Warlord. --- I'll give you anything you desire."

"Never!"

"You won't be able to save the girl. --- Just like you couldn't save him," the Master said as he pointed his sword toward Bill.

"What are you talking about?" my dark friend asked with furrowed eyebrows.

"You know exactly what I'm talking about. You killed him. It was your fault. Your guilt is a cancer that eats you from the inside. You killed him, and then you killed your wife and daughter because you were too weak to protect them."

Confused, I glanced at Bill, hoping he had an explanation, but he refused to look at me. Instead, he continued staring at the Master. A fury rose inside of me, causing a tidal wave of emotions to run through my body. A door opened in my mind, and I sensed that something was trying to come through. Quickly, I rushed to the door and blocked it with all my might. The door strained, but I would not bend to its merciless power. With one final push, I slammed it closed.

My dark friend screamed and rushed forward, sword up high for a killing blow. As the blade came down, the Master sidestepped, spun, and with the flat of his sword, he hit my friend in the back of his head. All went dark...

Katie Looks For Help

The sewer opened into a much larger section with deep water and walkways along the edge. Katie cleared the four steps that led to the path on her right and continued as fast as her tired legs could move. A stream of light appeared ahead, and she realized there was an uncovered manhole a mere one hundred yards in the distance. A ladder ran along the wall showing her the way to freedom.

Ignoring exhaustion and pain, the girl ran with renewed vigor. Just when things had seemed so grim, she could now see her salvation at hand. Then she heard the splash. She turned her head quickly, throwing off her balance, and nearly toppled into the dark waters below. She didn't see the monster immediately, but then she made out its head just above the water. Menacingly, she could see its gigantic tail slashing back and forth, propelling it through the water at breathtaking speed.

Fear and unflinching determination caused the young girl to push her body faster, if that was even possible. Her heart pounded so hard that it felt like it had risen into her throat, looking for a way to escape the torture she was putting it through. She was only a few feet from the ladder when the monster attacked. It leaped out of the murky waters, jaws open, reaching for its meal. Katie stared death in the face and surely would have been eaten if not for pure luck. At the last second, just as the creature's teeth were about to grab her, she tripped and fell flat on her stomach. The alligator's mouth snapped closed with a shuddering pop, just missing Katie, and the monstrosity slid back into the water.

Katie leaped up, grabbed the ladder, and quickly pulled herself up rung by rung. She dared not look down, but she heard the waters separate as the monster jumped again. At the same time, she grabbed the edge of the hole and yanked herself out onto the concrete. The ground shuddered as the gigantic creature hit the ceiling of the sewer a split second too late.

Utterly depleted of energy, Katie rolled over on her back. Her chest extended and retracted, searching for the air she so desperately needed. She lay there for several minutes trying to regain her composure, playing the events of her escapade through the sewers in her mind. Then she heard voices and realized she had almost forgotten how dangerous of a predicament she currently faced. She was in the open, and anyone nearby would be able to see her.

The young girl quickly scanned the area, and once again, luck was her friend. The sewer opening was surrounded by brick and rubble on all sides, blocking her from wandering eyes. Under her breath, she whispered, "Thank you, God," got on to her knees and peeked through an opening in the rubble. The street was filled with demons and slaves, but she recognized the area and realized it was only a few blocks from her final destination.

A demon was leading a group of slaves in a long, single-file line, and they were heading right past her position. *My only choice is to blend in.* She crawled around the edge of the rubble, looked both ways, stepped out, and simply followed the back of the line. All the slaves were chained together, but if she stayed close, then maybe no one would notice her. Actually, she had moved so quickly and quietly that the slave in front of her didn't even know she was behind him.

Shuffling along, she matched the steps of the slaves in line for another block. Demons leading other groups of slaves passed by, but so far, her ruse seemed to be working. They were more concerned about the slaves they were in charge of, or they simply never expected a free slave to try to stay in line with a captured group.

Then her group turned left at an intersection, only one block from where she needed to go. She was so close, but it seemed her good luck was running out. Then Katie spotted an alleyway a mere fifty feet up on her right. If she could get to the alleyway, then she could continue moving in the correct direction for the necessary final block.

Demons and slaves were everywhere. *Should I risk it?* Even if a demon didn't see her, maybe a slave would, and they could report her in order to gain favor. She could wait for a better opportunity, but what if that never came? The alleyway was tantalizingly only a few feet ahead and about ten feet to the right. It almost seemed alive as the dark shadows called to her, inviting her to enter. *What should I do?*

Once again, she asked God to guide her steps. She knew if she moved too quickly, then she would stand out and surely attract attention. Taking a deep breath, she slowly turned and continued to shuffle head down toward the alley. Those few steps seemed to last an eternity, as she imagined a million eyes watching her, but step by step, she grew closer to her goal, and no sound of alert was heard.

At a snail's pace, Katie continued her shuffling, zombie-like strides until the shadows invited her into safety, and she didn't stop this pace until she was several yards into the alley. Then the girl finally dared to turn and looked behind her. No one was coming, and no one had seen her. She thanked the Lord once again and moved off down the alley.

Katie was forced to move slowly as the alley was nearly pitch black. Night had fallen, and what little sunlight was available during the day had now left until the morning. She thought the sewers were dark, but at least there, she could use her lighter. There was no way she could risk using it here, out in the open.

The girl kept her one hand on the wall to the left and her other hand stretched out toward the front. She had heard stories of people being blind before the Last War and imagined this must be how it felt. She had never seen a blind person, and her parents told her that humans with disabilities were the first ones killed by the demons. This also included the sick or the elderly. If you couldn't work, then the demons felt you were useless.

Katie shuffled through the shadows, fingers rubbing the cool, grainy brick, while her opposite hand waved through the air like she was swatting bugs. Sometimes she would stub her feet on bricks and rubble, but luckily her shoes were relatively new and provided some protection.

At one point, her front hand encountered something hard and cold. She couldn't be sure, but it felt like steel. It was pushed up against the alley wall on the left, so she started to follow it out to her right. She followed along, keeping both hands on the obstacle until she hit the right wall of the alley. Her path was blocked, so she reached up as high as possible but only felt smooth, cold steel. Moving back to her left, the young girl slid her hands up and down, looking for something to grab so that she could climb over the obstacle, but the only reward she received was failure.

Argh, --- I'll have to retrace my steps and find another way. Katie exhaled, and then the thought popped into her mind. She dropped to her belly, and a ray of hope appeared before her. With her face to the ground, she could discern a flicker of light in the distance. Reaching her hand forward, she moved some of the rocks out of the way and could clearly see torch lights ahead. They were only a few hundred feet away, and their brightness revealed the end of the alleyway.

The space between the floor and the steel obstruction was only a couple of inches, but as she looked through narrowed eyes to her right, she could tell the gap widened. She crawled along on her stomach, and with every inch she moved, she felt the space grow larger and larger. Reaching the right alley wall, she realized the gap was about the same size as the sewer drain she had fit through earlier. *I can make it.*

The young girl reached in with her arm as far as possible and cleared out any debris in the way. Lying her head down, she started to worm her way through the opening inch by inch. The space was slightly bigger than the sewer drain, and in no time whatsoever, she reached the other side.

Once she was free of the obstruction, Katie quickly covered the remaining distance to the end of the alley and carefully looked in both directions. Her destination was the factory she had worked at last month. It stood across the street surrounded by a chain-link fence, and the torches she had seen earlier were at the front gate where two demons stood watch. If nothing had changed over the last month, then only one more demon stood watch inside the building at the rear entrance.

Katie's predicament was getting past the chain-link fence. She could easily climb over it, but she needed to get to the side or rear of the property. The two demon guards were just a little bit to her left, so if she stepped out of the alley, she would be in plain sight and easily captured. *I need a distraction.*

Katie pondered in the alleyway, but each new idea was tossed away as soon as it appeared. First, she thought about throwing rocks to make the demons look in a different direction. However, due to the proximity of the fence and the angle the alley allowed, she didn't think that was plausible. Every idea that came to her after that was even worse. *How can I come so far and yet be denied?* Sitting huddled with her back against the cold brick, her knees tucked to her chest, frustration clawed deep into her mind. She thought about Angelica and her warrior friend and wondered if they were even still alive. *I can't give up hope. There must be a way.*

Then she felt the first drop. It landed on her arm, and she watched it as it gingerly wound a path down her body, letting gravity pull it to the ground. Then another fell and another. The sky opened its flood gates, and the rain poured down unchallenged. It raced to the earth like a crazed army, hungry for battle. The thunder and lightning followed, unleashing its torment on those who listened both far and near. Humanity was powerless as nature unfurled itself with all its might.

Katie hadn't eaten or drank in almost a day, so she opened her mouth and quenched her thirst with the cool, refreshing water. Then she peeked around the corner, looking toward the demon guards. She couldn't see them. As a matter of fact, she couldn't see anything. The torrent was so powerful that it seemed like the fabric of reality had been twisted, changing dry land into a world meant for sea life. Her eyes could only see a few feet in front of her, blinded by the fury of the storm. *This is my chance. If I can't see the demons, then they can't see me.*

Springing up, she dashed across the street, feet sloshing as the water had already reached the height of the curb and began to overflow onto the sidewalk. The rain blinded her so much that she misjudged her distance and nearly crashed into the fence. Fortunately, she stopped herself at the last second without making any noise.

Clutching the chain-link rings, Katie began to use the fence as a guide, moving along its edge until she had worked herself to the back of the property. Once there, she dug her fingers even deeper into the metal links and started to scale the fence like a monkey. Her gym shoes slipped on the wet steel, but eventually, she climbed over and reached the other side unannounced.

As soon as Katie was inside the fence, the rain started to let up, so she needed to be careful. There was still at least one demon inside the factory that required her concern. The girl cautiously made her way toward the back of the building, keeping her eyes and ears open.

With soft steps, she reached the back outer wall, pressing

herself up against the wet aluminum sheeting. The large entrance to the back of the factory loomed to her right. It was a huge doorless opening, more than twenty feet wide and at least twelve feet high. Katie kept her back against the outer wall and slowly slid closer until she reached the edge of the entrance. With one eye, she peered around the corner and saw that the guard was only a few feet away. The creature sat in a wooden chair, back against the inner wall, and its head slumped on its chest. Loud, guttural snores emanated from its mouth. Katie breathed a sigh of relief.

Taking a quick scan across the room, she could see nearly one hundred slaves spread out across the factory floor, lying on the ground deep in slumber. Quietly tip-toeing her way in, she made her way past the guard and entered the factory.

Katie moved silently amongst the slaves, recognizing most of their faces as she passed. This had been her new family after her parents died. She had been placed here shortly after their deaths, and her friends here had given her a new purpose, especially the man in charge. Unfortunately, last month she had lost her newfound family when the demons relocated her to the village where Angelica had found her.

Katie's face beamed as she passed her friends. She wanted to wake them up so she could find out what had occurred since she had left, but the girl knew she had more important things to attend to first. She needed to speak to the man who could help her and Angelica. At this factory, he was the foreman overseeing the slaves, and he was the one who had helped her after the death of her parents. His teachings had given her new hope and a sense of direction. Katie could see him ahead, sitting on the floor with his legs crossed, deep in meditation.

Not wanting to disturb him, she covered the remaining distance on stealthy footsteps. The girl silently knelt in front of him. She nibbled at her lower lip as she prepared to speak, but before her mouth could open, the man spoke first, "It is good to see you again, Katie."

And Seng Shan opened his eyes...

Guilt

"My fake ID didn't work," I said with frustration as I came out of the liquor store.

"Crap! How are we going to get the girls to loosen up without wine coolers?" Bill asked.

"Don't worry. They'll loosen up plenty when they see my car."

"That's true. We should write chick magnet right here on the door."

I chuckled at that and responded, "I don't think my dad would be very happy about that."

We opened the doors and sunk into the car. It was weird sitting this low. My father only let me drive it on the weekends, and my own car was so much higher off the ground. I started up the engine and felt the power reverberate through the vehicle. A Corvette could give anyone confidence, and confidence was something I always lacked, at least with girls. It was funny how I could be so confident when it came to the martial arts, but with girls, I just locked up and couldn't open my mouth. It was almost like I could flip a switch when it came to my kung fu training.

All my friends said they could never imagine me getting into a fight, but once they did see me, they never doubted me again. They had a nickname for me – Richie Cunningham. Yes, the nice guy from "Happy Days." However, on the few occasions when my buttons had been pushed, and I had to defend myself, I had shown that other side of me. Honestly, it scared me when the other guy came out. In those instances, I became cold and uncaring, and it took all my effort to prevent me from really hurting someone.

It was funny how Bill and I were such opposites. He couldn't fight his way out of a paper bag, but when it came to speaking to the ladies, he was a master. Bill wasn't the best-looking guy in the world. He was short, at least six inches shorter than me, but he would never admit it. His body was as thin as a hockey stick, muscles almost non-existent, topped off by a pointy nose and bushy eyebrows, making him a long shot from being considered attractive. But something he could definitely do was get the girls laughing, and that's all it usually took.

So far, our senior year had been a blast. Every weekend Bill and I took the Corvette out, and every weekend we picked up girls. Between the 'Vette and Bill's antics, we were unstoppable. Earlier that day, we had met a couple of girls at the mall, and Bill used his usual charm to get us a date. We planned on picking them up when they got off work.

"Hey, pinhead! You're daydreaming again. Let's go, it's almost nine o'clock," Bill shouted over my car stereo.

"You're right," I replied as I backed up the Corvette and pulled out of the liquor store. Taking off down the street, Bill rolled down his window, stuck his head out, and screamed, "Here we come, ladies! We're coming to get you!"

Bill could be such a moron, but he was my best friend, and we had been inseparable ever since the summer before sixth grade. I still remember that day clearly. Baseball was my favorite sport, and this was my last year of Little League. Most people would say I was a pretty good player, and every year I was picked for the All-Star game. I was never known as a power hitter, but my average was always high, and I was extremely fast, stealing bases like a bank robber steals cash. Yet, I always dreamed of hitting a home run. It just never happened. I would hit the ball well, but I just never seemed to get under it.

Then my chance finally came. After five long years, I received the perfect pitch and matched it with a perfect swing. The ball moved like it had been shot from a rocket, flying into the gap between center and left field. There were no fences where we played, but if you hit the ball hard enough and it got past the outfield, it would surely be a home run. With a big grin on my face, I sprinted toward first, watching the ball sail with the corner of my eye. That's when I saw the center fielder furiously pumping his little legs, getting closer and closer to my home run. At the last second, he dived through the air, catching the ball in the web of his mitt, landing on his stomach, and sliding across the grass. All the parents and players from the other team went crazy, jumping and screaming like the boy had saved the world. Everyone was so excited, that is except for me. I couldn't believe he had made that catch.

When the game was over, I ran over to him and asked, "Why did you catch that fly ball? You robbed me of a home run."

"That's just what I do, man. Everything with style," Bill responded as he spun around with a dance move.

Laughing at his antics, we both gave each other high fives. From that moment on we became the best of friends. We hung out with each other constantly, and we learned every little secret about each other. I was the shy nerd who had a secret tougher side to me. He was Mr. Congeniality and Mr. Popular. Everyone liked Bill. The jocks liked him. The stoners liked him. The nerds liked him. And most of all, the girls liked him.

"Hey, dumb ass, snap out of it! You just passed a cop, and you're speeding!" Bill shouted.

"What?" I said as I came out of my daze and looked in my rearview mirror. Sure enough, the police car turned around and put its lights on. Crap, my father told me if I get one more ticket, he would never let me drive the Corvette again.

"What do I do?" I pleaded with Bill with doe-like eyes.

"Floor it!"

"I can't do that!"

"This car is too fast. He'll never catch you."

"I need to pull over."

"Don't be such a wimp! Stop being Mr. Rational, goodie-two-shoes, Richie Cunningham! If you get a ticket, we'll lose the Corvette!"

Glancing in the mirror again, I saw the cop closing the gap. My heart pounded like a ticking time bomb, sweat forming in every nook and cranny of my body. I can't lose the car. Wide-eyed, I looked at Bill again, his mouth moving in slow motion, forming the words for me to put the pedal to the floor. Sweat dripping from every pore, I shoved my foot down as hard as I could. The engine roared, throwing my back and head against the soft leather seat. The car launched like a catapult, flying effortlessly through the air and gravity as we shot down the road at blazing speed.

The speedometer went from fifty to eighty in the blink of an eye and continued to climb. Two cars appeared in front of us, driving side by side, blocking us from passing them. I had two choices, slow down or pass the double yellow line into oncoming traffic. My nails dug into the steering wheel as the sweat dribbled down my face. Should I give up and slow down?

Then something strange happened. Richie Cunningham decided to vacate my body, and I felt the other guy take over. The guy who had never lost a fight or a sparring match. The cold, uncaring person replaced me that didn't know the meaning of fear. Somehow, I was still there, watching from the outside, but he was the one driving, and I felt his reaction skills take over.

He quickly moved into the oncoming traffic, barely avoiding a semi-truck as it whizzed by, honking its horn. Passing the two cars, he slid back onto the right side of the road. All of this was done without reducing the speed or touching the brake. More cars loomed ahead, but they were no deterrent, as he continued to weave in and out with precise timing and impeccable skill. I knew I was the one doing it, but I couldn't believe how well I was driving. My face remained stoic, but inside I beamed with excitement. It felt like I was a professional race car driver.

While He or I made our race for the finish line, Bill went through several stages of emotion. At first, he laughed with glee, but when we made our reckless move into oncoming traffic, he screamed in fear. This only lasted for a second as he seemed to get control of his feelings and advised us on the next logical move.

"The cop's way behind us. Turn at the next light, and we'll lose him!" Bill shouted.

It seemed like a prudent move. The speedometer had passed one hundred and twenty, so I had to slow down fast, but the light was so close. We slammed on the brakes and probably could have made it if it wasn't for the weather. It had rained a few hours earlier, and this part of the street was still wet. The car started to spin, the back end twisting like a top, and we lost control. We tried to compensate, but the vehicle rotated a full 360 degrees, slid past the intersection, and came to an abrupt halt.

We looked in the mirror and saw the cop narrowing the distance. Gunning the accelerator, the wheels burned rubber, and the catapult launched once again. Another light loomed ahead, turning from yellow to red as we approached, but we didn't slow down.

"Stop!" Bill shouted.

I glanced at him and said, "We can't."

The car ran through the light, and in that fleeting moment, I felt Him abandon me, returning my control. The SUV plowed into the passenger side door, propelling the car to the left, as my head slammed into the side window. I blacked out for a minute and returned to consciousness, dazed and disoriented. The squad car lights are shining, causing my head to pound. The police officer is outside the car. He is pointing a gun at me and yelling something I can't make out. The fuzziness leaves my brain, and I look toward Bill. The door is crushed in against his body. He's pushed all the way against me, and his head hangs limply with his chin on his chest.

"Bill!" I shout.

"Wake up!" I scream.

The scene switches. I am walking the gauntlet of hatred, and I feel a hundred eyes upon me, stabbing their displeasure like hot knives, as I move between the mahogany wood aisles. So many beautiful flowers adorn the pulpit and the casket, but they do not comfort the hole in my heart.

Then I see them ahead to the right, sitting in the front row. For seven years I've known them, and during that span, I've been to their house a million times. They've taken me on vacation with them. They've told me I'm like another son to them.

Now I'm standing before them, and she rises, bringing her watery eyes to look into mine. It's only been a few days since I last saw her, but she has aged so much. She looks pale and sickly as the tears roll down her face and puncture my heart. I want her to hug me. I want her to forgive me. Instead, she pulls back her hand and slaps me across the face. The sting penetrates me completely.

The sound of dripping turns my eyes to the casket. Crimson flows out of it, soaking the carpet. It rolls down the aisle like a broken dam, filling the pews. Bill sits up in the coffin and looks at me with zombie eyes. He is covered in blood, a piece of flesh hanging off his face.

He opens his mouth and says, "I should never have caught that fly ball."

Waking from the nightmare, I find my arms tied above me. The rope is attached from the ceiling to my wrists, and the length has been made so my toes barely touch the ground. My shoulders ache, and my arms are numb, except for little phantom pin-pricks dancing across my nervous system. Turning my head left and right, I see the big guy and Bill hanging next to me in the same unpleasant situation.

I look at Bill and say, "I just had the weirdest dream about you."

"Oooh, you're turning me on. Are you sure it was a

dream?"

I think about this for a second and realize I cannot answer. Was it a dream? I've been so confused lately that I don't know what reality is anymore. All I know for sure is we have to escape, and we must save Angelica.

The Power Of An Angel

Angelica stood near the windows, looking out at the city below. Her hands remained bound behind her back, and her mouth was still gagged. The demons had locked her in a smaller room two floors down from the Master's penthouse.

Thinking about her encounter with the Master, she couldn't understand how her friend could have been so easily fooled by the monster. She could see the real horror that he was. *Why can't my friend see it?* But maybe she was the only one who did understand. Something had changed in her recently, a feeling brewing deep down inside, waiting to escape.

With all that had transpired recently, she hadn't found time to think about her capture in the alley. *How did I know that prayer could hurt them?* She remembered that feeling calling to her, or maybe it was a voice in her head that told her to pray. The feeling was pure. It was light and love bound together in a never-ending bond that was inseparable. Most importantly, she realized that it hadn't left her. If she concentrated, she could feel the power pulsing inside her body, ready to be unleashed.

Angelica remembered the look on the Master's face when he heard her voice. Fear washed over his countenance, and he knew that she could hurt him with the word of God. She needed to escape and help her friend before the Master killed him. For all she knew, he could already be dead, but the more she thought about it, she knew that wasn't true. Somehow, she could sense he was still alive.

The young girl used her new-found power and reached out with her mind. A path opened before her, showing her the way, sending her ghostly essence through the hallways, past doors, and open rooms until finally, she stood in front of him. He was dreaming, eyes rapidly fluttering, sweat rolling down his skin as his body occasionally gave off a spastic shake. But it was more than just a dream. --- It was a nightmare. Angelica felt his suffering and wanted so badly to awaken him. Reaching with her specter-like hand, she entered his mind. The memories of his friend Bill, lying lifeless in the car, were thrust into the girl's thoughts. Then a split second of blackness, and she was at the funeral. She watched as Bill's mother drew her hand back. The slap knocked her to the floor, returning her from the ghost walk.

Crumpled on the ground, she touched her cheek and felt the stinging pain and her dark friend's misery deep inside her soul. The tears poured from her eyes, and it was several minutes before she regained her composure. As she rocked back and forth on the cold floor, it dawned upon her that she wasn't the only one who could see her friend's thoughts. The Master could also see them, and that's why he hadn't killed him. He uses your guilt against you, and he would try to turn her friend into a weapon for himself. *I must stop him.*

Angelica focused once again, but this time her ghostly apparition floated upward through the ceiling, stopping at the next floor. Moving through the hallways, she explored every room until finally, she was rewarded. Marching on its patrol, a demon guard walked straight toward her. She entered its body, reaching into the darkest crevices of its mind. She hoped there was something human left, but all that remained was a twisted, empty vessel. If any flame of goodness had existed, it had long ago been extinguished. There was no way she could save the creature, but maybe that wasn't necessary. *All I need to do is control it.*

The girl furrowed her eyebrows, sending subtle commands toward the demon, telling it to come to her room. The monster stopped moving, and she felt the barrier of resistance rise up, attempting to block her request. Defiantly, the demon said, "No!" and she realized that the power to command was beyond her limits. *So be it! If I can't command him, then I'll punish him.* The girl began to recite the Lord's Prayer once again, and immediately the monster dropped to the floor in torment. She stopped her prayer and whispered in its mind, "Come to my room now, or I'll continue."

The demon lay on the ground on all fours panting heavily, and after several breaths, the creature said, "I'll come to your room and kill you, you little witch!"

"That's fine, just hurry up. I don't have all day," Angelica responded in a calm, soothing voice.

Staying in the creature's mind, she traveled with it as it ran down the hallway, descended the stairs, and in no time whatsoever reached her doorway. It stood there for several seconds, contemplating its next move. Angelica could feel the fear as it entered the demon's mind, and she realized she would need to give the monster a little extra shove.

"Don't tell me you're afraid of a little girl. What will everyone else think when I tell them how much of a coward you are?" Angelica spoke into its mind.

The demon became enraged, opened the door, barged into the room, and drew a long knife from its scabbard. The creature rushed toward Angelica screaming, hoping its cries would break the girl's concentration.

But this was no longer the scared little girl who had hidden in the basement. This was an avenging angel who had watched as demons slaughtered her parents. As the monster entered, Angelica remained calm and transferred her prayer into the demon's mind. The creature dropped the knife and fell to the floor, both hands grasping its head as it rolled back and forth in agony. She continued pushing her prayer deep into the demon's thoughts, repeating the blessed words over and over.

The monster started bleeding from its eyes and ears, and then its body began to shake violently, legs and arms flailing in every direction. Finally, after one tremendous convulsion, it stopped moving and lay lifeless on the tile floor.

Angelica finished her prayer and thanked God for the gift he had given her. Dropping to the floor where the knife had fallen, she scooted backward until she could grab the weapon. Holding the blade handle with her fingers, she started moving it back and forth across her bindings. It was tedious work, but after what seemed like an eternity, she was finally free.

Yanking the gag from her mouth, she felt the soreness on her lips and gums. The demon had a water bottle hanging at its waist, so she quickly snatched it and poured the contents into her mouth. The cool water was refreshing, alleviating the pain, so she swished it around with her tongue and swallowed. Her voice worked again, and this renewed her faith. It was her weapon, after all, and it was time for battle.

Angelica left the room behind her and headed toward her dark friend. Reaching out with her ghost-like powers, she checked to see if any demons would be in her path. As she did this, she sensed something in the opposite direction. Focusing intently, she turned and reached out farther until she found what she was looking for. There was a young boy imprisoned on the same floor that she was.

Heading back down the hallway, she moved past her room and toward the young boy. His room was the very last one on the left, just before the stairs. Reaching the door, she tried to turn the handle, but unfortunately, it was locked.

Angelica knocked on the door lightly and said, “Can you hear me?”

“Who are you?” the boy timidly asked from the other side.

“I’m Angelica, and I’ve come to help you. The door is locked. Do you know where the key is?”

"No, I don't."

Angelica pondered about this for a moment and said, "I think I know where it is. I'll be right back."

"Don't leave me! I've been alone for so long," the boy pleaded.

"It's okay. I promise you I'll come back," Angelica responded with true compassion in her voice as she turned and headed back toward her room.

Angelica sprinted down the hallway and entered her former prison. The demon still lay on the floor, face first and motionless. Dropping down next to the creature, she searched through its back pockets but to no avail. She would have to roll the demon over to search the front pockets. With great effort, she pushed and pulled, finally turning the creature over onto its back. Dead eyes stared up at her, and for a moment, she could imagine the monster coming back to life and grabbing her. A shiver ran down her spine, causing her body to shake, but it didn't deter her. She quickly slipped her hand into the first pocket, searching with her fingers, but she found nothing. Then she dug her hand into the last pocket and felt the metal key.

"There you are," she exclaimed with a smile as she removed the key and pressed it to her lips.

Angelica was up again and moving down the hallway. She reached the door and inserted the key, hearing the resounding click as she opened the door. A young oriental boy, approximately eleven years old, stood there with a smile on his face.

"Hi, I'm Fu," he said.

The Forging Of Steel

"Did the demons transfer you back to make swords once again?" asked the monk with a doubtful look.

"No, Da Shifu," Katie replied. "I escaped, and I've come here for your help."

Katie was starving, so Seng Shan shared some food with her as she told her story. She told the monk how she had almost been raped until a young girl named Angelica rescued her. Also, how Angelica was trying to save her warrior friend and his incredible exploits in battle before he was captured. Finally, she told him of her adventure in the sewers and how close she had come to becoming food for the giant alligator.

"This girl says her warrior friend killed hundreds of demons by himself?" asked the monk with a quizzical look on his face.

"Yes, Da Shifu."

"Do you believe her?"

"Yes, Da Shifu, I do. I know it seems impossible, but there is something special about this girl, and I know in my heart she's not lying. We have to help them."

The monk seemed to ponder this for a moment before saying, "It's not impossible. In my youth, I did things that many people would not be able to understand. Did you see this man she speaks of?"

"Only from a distance."

"What did he look like?"

"I was really far away, so I couldn't get a close look at him, but I could tell he's a white man with brown hair. It was hard to determine his size, but he might have been a little taller than yourself. Do you know him?"

"Maybe, it was a long time ago. Did this girl say anything about his tactics in battle?"

Katie thought about this for a few seconds but reluctantly responded, "I don't think so."

"Think hard, Katie. Did she say anything about his fighting style? Did he move like anything?"

"Yes! She said he move like a bird!"

Seng Shan smiled and said, "Not just any bird, an eagle. I know who this man is, and, yes, with his help, we can win. Start to wake everyone. The time has finally come for war."

Katie sprang to her feet, a smile exploding across her face at the thought of seeing her friends again. Sprinting around the building on padded feet, she roused the workers, putting a finger to her lips and telling them to gather in the center of the factory.

***

In the meantime, Seng Shan quietly walked over to the sleeping demon guard. In one deft move, his hand thrusted forward, and he tore the creature's throat out. The monster dropped to its knees, eyes bulging, hands clutching at the hole that had once been its throat, as the blood gurgled down its chest, forming a pool of red between it and the monk. The creature tried to speak but only spit up blood before it splashed forward into the crimson pond it had created. Looking at the demon lying before him, Seng Shan knew there was no turning back now.

The monk went to the back corner of the building and retrieved his sword from the armory, and then he snuck outside the factory, quiet as a mouse. There was a small, dilapidated shack about fifty yards away, next to the opening at the front gate. Seng Shan stealthily moved across the muddy ground, covering the distance until he squatted next to the building. Both demon guards had moved inside the building when the storm had started, and the monk could see them through the window, huddled together in the corner, sound asleep.

With cat-like silence, he slowly opened the door and entered the shack. The demon to his right was snoring loudly, deep in sleep. The demon to his left started to stir and opened its eyes. The last thing the monster saw was the sword as it entered its chest. Seng Shan removed the weapon and looked at the other demon. It still sat their snoring away, oblivious that death was so near until the monk plunged his sword into its heart.

Seng Shan left the shack, wiping the blood from his sword as he returned to the factory. By this time, Katie had woken the slaves, and they had retrieved all the weapons they could carry from the armory. The monk called his army to the center of the building. They crowded in, creating a circle around him and Katie. Many of Katie's old friends hugged her and welcomed her back as they waited for the monk to speak.

The monk scanned the room, making eye contact with each and every one of his followers. Clearing his throat, he said, "The time has finally come. Your training is over, and it is time for you to seek revenge against the evil that has plagued us for so long."

Seng Shan paused and forcefully said, "I will not lie to you. The path you choose will not be easy. Many of you will die today, but I can make you this promise. Your deaths will never be forgotten! Your names will live on through the centuries as we change history and reclaim this world!"

The people howled and stomped their feet in unison...

"We will move from one camp to the next, freeing our people and recruiting others to join our fight. Everyone will carry two swords, and as we add to our army, give the extra swords to others. --- Our enemy has grown lazy and complacent. They do not expect us to be so strong, and that is their weakness. --- We are as strong as the steel we forged!"

More shouting from the army...

"Does steel feel pain!" the monk screamed.

"No, Da Shifu!" the army shouted.

"Does steel feel fear!"

"No, Da Shifu!"

"Then become steel and cut deep into their hearts!"

The army fanatically howled and hooted...

Seng Shan appreciated their exuberance and let the army have a few moments to build their morale, but then he calmed them, for stealth would now be of the utmost importance. There was still an hour of darkness left, and they would use this to their advantage to surprise the enemy. They left the building like assassins in ninja-like silence.

Escape

My eyes open, cloudy, and disoriented. Looking up, I find my arms tied above me, and the rope is attached from a steel beam in the ceiling to my wrists. The length of the rope has been made, so my toes barely touch the ground. My shoulders ache, and my arms are numb, except for little phantom pin-pricks dancing across my nervous system. Turning my head left and right, I see the other guy and Bill hanging next to me in the same unpleasant situation. They're talking about some stupid dream.

The pain must be excruciating for them, but I won't let it bother me. I'm used to pain, and I know how to control it. I refuse to let it defeat me, for if I do, Angelica will suffer, and that I will not allow. Escape and saving her are all that matter. Pain can wait until later.

Grabbing the rope with my hands, I grit my teeth and try to pull myself up. The strain on my muscles is incredible. It feels like a million hot needles are being stabbed into my flesh, and I try to block it out, but no matter how hard I concentrate, the misery returns. However, I will not yield. Screw pain!!!

As I continue to pull upward, I can barely hear Bill and the other guy yelling out words of encouragement. I wish they would just shut the hell up! They're messing with my concentration, preventing me from blocking out the searing agony burning through my biceps. Bright spots flash in front of my eyes as the pain attempts to drain my will, but losing it is not something I will allow. I am the master of my mind and body, and victory is the only thing I will accept.

Resolutely, I continue to pull until finally, I create enough slack. Using my abdominal muscles, I throw my legs forward and up, completely inverting my body. Wrapping my legs around the rope, I relieve the stress on my arms. Even though some of the pain is gone, my arms still throb, and I fear that I may have torn a muscle, but I can't worry about that now.

By holding my weight with my legs, I can now bring my wrist to my mouth. My teeth tear in, ripping at the rope like a hungry animal. It is a painstakingly slow process, but little by little, I gnaw away and come closer to my goal.

The minutes pass as I continue to eat my way toward freedom. My arms feel much better, but the pain has only traded places with my legs and jaw. The pain in my legs is starting to disappear, but that's only because I'm losing feeling in them. I purposely have to squeeze them together every once in a while, just to make sure I don't lose grip on the rope.

My jaw and the back of my neck are on fire, and they plead with me to stop. They beg me to give up, promising relaxation and peace, but I only want pain. I dig in and deny them their triumph. Angelica's face appears in my mind, and I am renewed with determination, so I continue nibbling away like a starving mouse and force the pain from my body. I will not yield!

Little by little, the rope strands tear away. Sweat rolls down my back, dripping to the floor as it forms a puddle beneath me. My whole body is soaked in perspiration, and the moisture leaks into my eyes, momentarily blinding me, causing me to wipe them periodically.

I don't know how much time has passed. The concept of time becomes meaningless, as my mind and body become attuned to only one desire - escape. A huge hole is now discernible in my bindings, and I begin to flex my arm muscles back and forth, trying to twist my wrist. A few strings snap. It's working!

My teeth burrow in once again, tearing and twisting with renewed enthusiasm. At the same time, I flex my arms violently with every ounce of strength I can muster. More strings snap, teasing me with absoluteness. A chuckle erupts in my throat, trapping itself behind my teeth, causing a growl-like sound of a man or monster losing his sanity. Finally, with one last yanking motion, the rope breaks and I am free.

Overjoyed, I momentarily lose concentration and almost forget to hold on to the rope with my hands and legs, causing me to slip a few inches before catching hold. Then I slowly lower my legs to the floor. The feeling is gone below my waist, and as soon as my feet touch the surface, my body collapses.

My legs are useless ghostly apparitions. If anyone entered the room right now, I would be easy prey, so I roll over and start to rub my legs with my hands, hoping the circulation will return. The feeling begins to come back slowly, but as it does, I regret my efforts. The pain is unbearable. It feels like a cactus is being rolled back and forth across my thighs, causing mini explosions of agonizing discomfort.

This is taking too long, and I need to hurry up before someone comes to check on us. Kneading my palms into my thighs, I continue rubbing rapidly until the pain begins to lessen. Then I try to get up, but immediately my body falls back to the floor. It takes me several tries, but I'm finally able to stand on spaghetti legs.

"Hurry up and free us!" shouts Bill.

"The mirror in the bathroom!" shouts the other guy.

Limping to the bathroom, I push open the door. Holding the sink with my left hand, I smash the mirror with my fist, causing the shards of glass to tumble onto the sink counter. One of the pieces is long and sharp like a dagger and should do the job. Grabbing the piece, I move back to my companions, and as I do this, I notice my legs are finally starting to return to semi-normal. It's easy to cut through their bonds, and when I'm finished, I begin searching the room for a weapon as they massage out the pain in their arms.

Unfortunately, the room is barren, and I can't remotely find anything I can turn into an instrument that will inflict any harm. That's alright; my hands will do just fine. I won't make the same mistake as last time and allow him to get into my head. This time he'll die! They'll all die! Wait --- I won't lose control again. I need to keep focused on Angelica. She's my priority, and I need to find her. They'll be plenty of time for killing later.

Our trio leaves the room, and we enter a long hallway with several double doors on each side. We check each room as we move along, opening the doors and peering inside. They are all exactly like the room we were imprisoned in, but unfortunately, there is no sign of Angelica.

We are just about to reach the end of the hallway and a cross-section to the left when I hear somebody or something coming. We put our backs to the wall and nudge forward to the edge of the cross-section. It's a demon. I've killed enough of them to recognize that horrible stench.

Drawing my right fist back, I prepare to attack. As the creature rounds the corner, I launch my fist forward with precise accuracy. There is a look of horror on the demon's face as my fist crushes his breastbone and smashes his heart. The monster lets a small wheezing breath escape its mouth before it drops dead on the carpet floor.

My companions and I search the body for weapons, but the only thing we find is a short dagger. It will have to do for now. We find ourselves in a large open area approximately fifty feet wide. Large glass windows cover the entire wall to our right, and they give us a clear view of the outside as they rise from the floor to the ceiling. Elaborate sofas and chairs cover the entire area, but I cannot fathom what purpose they serve.

We move across the room, but as we approach the other side, we once again hear something coming from the hallway.

We flatten ourselves against the wall, and this time unlike the last, I have the dagger ready for action.

The footfalls of two individuals enter my ears, but they're very light, and then I smell her sweet fragrance. Putting the knife down, I quickly round the corner. Angelica and a young Chinese boy are staring back at me. The boy is startled, but Angelica smiles at me and rushes forward, grabbing me fiercely in a deep hug.

An intense feeling of euphoria overcomes my being. She is safe, and this causes my trepidations to vanish. I squeeze her tightly, never wanting to let go again. The last five years of misery flash backward, and the pain disappears. She's alive! My little girl is alive! Wait --- that's not right. Pushing Angelica to arm's length, I look her over from head to toe. She looks like my daughter, but it's not her. My daughter is… Pain racks my head, and a door slams shut in my mind.

My hands shoot to my head as I drop slumped to the ground, trying to stop the throbbing stab of anguish that permeates my heart. Then I feel Angelica's hand on my head, and her comforting words echo in my mind. She tells me it's okay and to focus only on her voice. Her words soothe me, and my distress disappears.

I'm baffled at hearing her words in my head, but then again, everything lately has been so confusing, so I do not question her and simply say, "Thank you."

Then I get up, regaining my composure, and say, "It's time to finish this."

"I agree," Angelica replies as she introduces me to her new friend, and I shake his hand.

"It's nice to meet you. Stay close to us," I reply as we start to head back past the glass windows and toward the stairway. However, we all come to a sudden halt as something catches our eyes through the windows, far away in the distance.

"Holy crap!" Bill exclaims.

Rebellion

The army grew as it headed east through the city. Under the cover of darkness, they had already attacked five different camps without being noticed. All the demon guards had been killed, and what had started as ninety-five brave souls had now swelled to nearly six hundred.

Not one human had stayed behind. Their hatred for demons was all the inspiration they needed to fight. All the straight swords had been passed out, so the youngest captors were sent back to the armory to retrieve the remaining stock. All told, there were nearly four hundred swords now in the hands of the former slaves. The rest of the men, women, and children found whatever weapons they could. Some found steel pipes or pieces of wood; others simply picked up bricks or rocks as they made their way down the streets of Houston.

It was daylight by the time they reached the sixth work camp, and unfortunately, this was where they were finally unveiled. Four demons were guarding the camp, two at the rear and two in the front. This camp was a food distribution center, and the slaves were already up, preparing for incoming wagons from the nearby farms.

The monk quietly led a small group of ten men to dispatch the demons as they had at the five previous camps. Five of them went toward the back, while the monk and the others headed toward the front of the compound. The rest of the army stayed back several hundred feet, hiding behind a large building and waiting for instructions.

Taking great care with each step, Seng Shan's small group made their way around the chain-link fence that surrounded the building. Several cars were still parked along the sidewalk's edge from days long past. All of them roasted completely black, both inside and out, a lasting reminder of the firestorm from the nuclear blast. The heat had melted their tires into liquid, gravity pulling the substance to the edge of the street, where the sidewalk steps up, and then eventually cooling, creating a hardened layer of rubber down the street's edge.

The group with Seng Shan was still two hundred yards from the front entrance when they heard screams inside the factory.

"The other party must have been discovered," Katie whispered.

"And we're not in position to attack the front entrance yet," Seng Shan replied as he pursed his lips and exhaled.

The two demons guarding the front were now on the alert. One of the demons dashed back inside the building, which is precisely what Seng Shan had hoped. He had wanted to keep the demons inside the compound and prevent their escape. But the other demon that remained at the front gate wouldn't be so easily fooled. The creature continued to vigilantly scan the area in all directions. Seng Shan and his team were forced to hide behind an old truck to prevent themselves from being seen.

The demon that had gone inside soon came back, running at full speed, with more than a hundred slaves in pursuit, frantically screaming and shouting. The monk knew now that stealth would no longer exist, and he spurred his group toward the front gate as rapidly as they could run. The demon guard who had remained at the front saw them coming, and without thinking twice, the creature bolted away.

Seng Shan knew they couldn't catch him, so instead, they

turned their attention to the other demon. It was a race to the front entrance, and it looked like the creature was going to be victorious. The monster shot through the opening with the monk still twenty yards away. Seng Shan pulled a small blade from his sleeve, brought his right hand back, and launched it with all his might. The weapon flew through the air, finding its mark, lodging itself in the demon's neck.

The creature took another step, blood showering from its artery, then it stumbled and fell to the floor dead. The human slaves were upon the demon instantly, kicking and tearing at the body, before Seng Shan arrived, jumped into the melee, and separated them.

"We are better than that!" the monk shouted. "I know you hate them, but we will not lower ourselves to their level and desecrate their bodies!"

By this time, Seng Shan's warriors who had attacked the rear of the building had arrived. They informed him that one of their group had died in the fighting. This was the first casualty of the war, and Seng Shan took the news badly. Nevertheless, they must press on, so he called for the rest of the army to join him so that he could have a word with the troops.

It took several minutes for everyone to gather on the street outside the building. The monk looked over the group, which now consisted of more than seven hundred souls, and shouted, "The time for surprise is over! They will be ready for us! The true fighting begins now!"

The army howled as they raised their weapons in the air…

"We form two lines, all those with swords on the front line! We march to the tower until they're all dead!"

The army screamed vehemently for several seconds. Then they spread out and formed two lines as they had been instructed. Katie joined Seng Shan at the front center as they started to move off, marching down the streets of Houston and heading toward the tower. Death or freedom waited for them in the distance.

The Battle For Houston

Abraham was overseeing developments at a new camp, just south of the tower, when the word came to him. At first, he assumed that the demon who told him of a slave rebellion was exaggerating. However, after sending out several scouts, he realized the truth. This was no minor rebellion. The monk had betrayed him and formed an army of somewhere between five hundred and a thousand soldiers.

Worse yet, they had the swords from the armory. As far as he could recall, there were nearly four hundred swords completed at last count, and his elite guard only had one hundred swords. This meant the only way to beat the monk was by sheer numbers, so he would have to gather his forces as soon as possible.

Without delay, he called for his elite guard and any other demons in the area to prepare for battle. Most importantly, he sent a demon to the tower to recover his ace in the hole. *Seng Shan's grandson will put a stop to this war, or he will die a miserable death.* Hopefully, the demon would bring young Fu to him before the battle started. Abraham wanted to put a stop to this rebellion without any bloodshed. He could care less about the slaves themselves, but he didn't want the output of work to decrease.

Gathering his army around him, Abraham mounted his horse, and they made their way to the open area in front of the tower. The landscape was flat and desolate, leaving no advantage of terrain or cover. Patiently, he waited as more and more demons came to join him, and within one hour, his forces had grown to more than two thousand. A broad smile crossed his face as he viewed the troops and realized the mighty power he wielded. *If I can't stop this peacefully, I'll crush them.*

It wasn't long before Abraham could hear Seng Shan's army approaching. The footsteps pounded a rhythmic drum beat as dust rose in the distance. The army reached the top of the crater, pausing for a brief moment. Then they moved down the slope, heading toward Abraham, howling and screaming. Abe swore under his breath and wondered if the monk's grandson would get there in time.

◆ ◆ ◆

Our faces were splattered against the glass windows with a look of awe and amazement. An army of humans was marching across the open terrain toward the tower. How could this be? I turned a questioning eye toward Bill and was just about to speak when Angelica answered my question.

"It's your grandfather," she said to Fu as a smile crossed her face from ear to ear. "My friend Katie went to get him."

"I knew he would come," Fu joyously replied.

"Look at the demon army. They outnumber them three to one," our dark friend stated. "They'll never win."

"I can help them," Angelica said.

"No, you can't," our dark companion replied. "You're just a little girl, and I'm too far away to make it there in time. The only way to stop them is to kill the Master. Stay here. I'm going up to face him."

Angelica grabbed his hand and pleaded, "No! You can't beat him without me! --- If you go, you'll die! I can't save you and

Katie at the same time!"

"You saved me the day I met you. Now it's my turn," he replied.

Our dark friend disengaged himself from her grip, and we headed toward the stairway. Just before we entered the stairwell, Bill turned back toward Angelica. She was looking at us with tears in her eyes.

Bill said, "Don't worry, my friend is really hard to kill."

The door closed, and Angelica screamed, "Don't listen to him!" unsure if he had heard her plea…

◆ ◆ ◆

Seng Shan and the army reached the edge of the crater. With a quick scan, the monk could see that the army he faced outnumbered him three to one. Luckily, his original ninety-three students, including Katie, still remained, and all of them had been personally trained by him. *I'll rely heavily on their prowess.* He had placed all of them on the front lines, splitting them into three groups. The first group was in the center with him, while the other two guarded the flanks.

Abraham would surely try to outflank him with his superior numbers, and that he could not allow. He realized that four hundred men shoulder to shoulder would not cover the crater's diameter in the center. This would make it easy for Abraham to hold him off while sending other soldiers around his flanks. *Our best bet is a V-formation.* His flanks would only go forward as far as they could while remaining close to the edge of the crater. This would prevent Abraham from getting around him and surrounding his army. Seng Shan would pierce forward in the center like a sharp sword, and if needed, the center could retreat backward and draw the enemy to them. With this tactic, Abraham's numbers wouldn't matter. He would only be able to engage them one-on-one.

Still, the demon army's main advantage would be their soldiers in reserve. The monk's people would have to outlast them with will and endurance. He only hoped that the man Katie mentioned could help them in time.

Fu, are you still alive?

Seng Shan thought about what the monsters had done to his wife and daughter, and his forearm flexed, causing him to dig his fingers into the grip of his sword. *Today is the day I avenge my family, and if I die in the process, then so be it. I've been ready for death ever since they died, but before my life force leaves this world, I'll make sure to kill as many of these evil creatures as possible.*

At his order, the army moved down the crater's edge, and he directed them into the V-formation. Moving in unison, they marched forward into a valley of shadow.

◆ ◆ ◆

From his vantage point, Abraham could see how the monk's army had moved into a V-formation, marching toward him as they entered the crater. He knew the monk was clever and realized this tactic would prevent him from flanking their army. The only way Abraham could flank them was to move some of his soldiers outside of the crater and then come around from behind. The problem was the monk would surely see this and compensate. Abraham decided the best course was to only send a few soldiers out of the crater and have them recruit other demons in the city to attack from the rear. But this could take time, and there was no guarantee they would return before the battle was over.

Time was of the essence, and Abe's best alternative would be remaining patient and waiting as long as he could. If Seng Shan's grandson was brought before him, he could possibly prevent the war. If not, then he needed the time for more recruits to return. *I can't fail and disappoint the Master.* He kept his army ready, but time was running out.

◆ ◆ ◆

From a thousand feet up, Angelica watched the scene below, her heart racing, palms sweating. She needed to help them, but they were so far away. *But are they far?* Something had seemed strange to her ever since she had entered the tower. It was the same feeling she had when she met the Master. Thinking back, she tried to focus, remembering the details of what she had seen. It wasn't just the Master that had changed to his true form. His penthouse suite had also changed. When she first entered the room, elaborate and expensive furniture filled the area. Beautiful paintings decorated the walls, and everything was crisp and immaculately clean. It wasn't until she looked upon the master that the truth was revealed. Broken glass, bent steel, and fractured concrete littered the floor. *Everything in that room was a façade.*

She turned to Fu and said, "I'm going to help them. Stay here."

"How can you help them? --- We're on the seventy-third floor. You'll never make it in time."

"Everything here isn't as it seems," she replied as she walked toward the stairwell.

Angelica focused her mind and tried to remember the feeling she had experienced in the penthouse. Reaching out with her power, a warm feeling entered her being. The wall in front of her started to change color, melting away, losing substance. Floors and ceilings simply evaporated into nothingness. With new clarity, she opened the door to the stairwell and walked out onto the battlefield. The tower was gone.

◆ ◆ ◆

"Angelica said we shouldn't listen to him," I told my companions as we moved through the stairwell.

"No kidding, he's a manipulator," Bill replied and then said to our dark friend, "Big guy, don't let him get in your head again. Kill this scum bag just like all the others you've taken down!"

Our dark friend didn't say anything. He just continued moving up the steps until we reached the final floor. This is what the last five years had been all about. His revenge would be fulfilled. He would kill this evil monster, and we would finally be able to rest. Maybe we could find a small, quiet town, and all of us could watch Angelica grow to adulthood. Maybe my dark friend would finally be at peace.

Creeping to the door, we turned the doorknob and entered the penthouse. Everything looked the same as before, except the Master had some guests. Several beautiful women lay sprawled on the sofas, in the throes of passion, as they performed sexual acts on each other.

"Do you like my friends?" the Master asked as he walked out from behind the kitchen counter to our right.

"Oh, I definitely like them," Bill replied as he stared with his mouth wide open.

"Remember what Angelica said, don't listen to him! He's trying to trick us!"

The Master moved behind one of the sofas and reached down, grabbing one of the women's breasts. Another woman started to kiss him vigorously, reaching down and grabbing his private parts. He separated, smiled, and said, "So sweet, they could be yours in any way that you want them."

"I have to admit it's tempting, but it looks like they get around," Bill replied. "I'd probably be scratching my groin for the rest of my life."

The Master laughed, looked at the women on the sofa, and said, "What a pity." Then he snapped his fingers, and they vanished. "I see that you've brought your friends again, or at least you think you brought them," he said with a chuckle. Then he walked within a few steps of my dark companion and asked, "Have you been able to stop the guilt you feel inside?"

"Don't listen to him!" I shouted.

"I can still help you. I can relieve your pain forever," the Master said.

"The only thing you can do for me is die," my dark friend answered as he lunged forward with his knife.

◆ ◆ ◆

Abraham couldn't wait any longer. They were almost upon him, so he deployed his elite guard to meet the point of the V head-on. At the same time, he sent the rest of his troops to attack the sides of the V formation, leaving only five hundred demons in reserve to protect himself.

The elite guard moved in with swords drawn, but before they could engage, the humans to the rear of the V formation peppered them with small rocks. Most of the projectiles missed, but some found their mark, tearing flesh and cracking bones. Two demons even dropped to the ground, never to rise again.

Then the two great armies met, with spirited screams echoing through the valley. Hundreds of swords fell upon hundreds of swords, creating a song of skill and perseverance. Blocks and parries moved up and down the lines, and blood filled the field of death.

◆ ◆ ◆

Seng Shan moved like a young man, rejuvenated by the thrill of battle. His sword deflected every strike, almost as if a magnet attracted it to the enemy's weapon. Katie stood behind him with a long, sharpened stick. Whenever the opportunity presented itself, she would lunge in, landing strikes to the enemy's legs and torso. Most of her strikes weren't lethal, but they were enough to distract or slow down the enemy. This was all Seng Shan needed as several elite guards met their doom under the combination of these two great heroes.

The monk had trained his students well, and after the first initial onslaught, over half of the elite guard lay dead on the battlefield. The human army had only lost five soldiers, and momentarily their spirits soared. Yet, this jubilance didn't last long. As each demon fell, another one immediately filled in the gap and continued their relentless push forward.

Those toward the back, who hadn't yet entered the fray, couldn't help but stand in amazement as they watched the eloquent skill of the warrior monk. They could only wonder how an old man could possibly move the way that he did. He sidestepped every attack as it attempted to knock on the doors of his defense, but the only answer it received was death from the point of his sword. He was a whirlwind of chaos, removing hands and arms at every opportunity, the limbs falling to the earth, creating a picket fence of the dead.

Blood filled the valley, trying to quench its thirst like a desert swallows up water. The warriors slipped on it like ice, falling to the ground, forced to slurp up its contents. Bodies on both sides continued to drop by the hundreds, only to be trampled by the ones behind them.

Thirsting for revenge, Seng Shan and his army fought on, but the tide began to turn, and they had no choice but to fall back. They still held their ranks, but more brave warriors continued to fall to the overwhelming odds. The V-formation collapsed back into a straight line, and the human warriors were forced to dig their heels in, fighting with desperate intensity. It appeared they were holding their own until cries of despair came from the backline.

There was a temporary lull in the battle, so the monk quickly turned to see what the commotion was, and the sight that hit him was like a hammer in his gut. More than a hundred demons were behind them coming down the crater's embankment.

◆ ◆ ◆

From the other side of the field, Abraham could see his recruits entering the crater behind the monk's army. He exhaled as a wicked smile lifted his cheek muscles. He had them surrounded and knew that the battle was his, so he spurred his horse forward with his reserves following close behind. *If I cannot stop the rebellion peacefully, then I'll make sure the slaves are punished and used as an example for those who would stand against the Master.* Abe commanded his men to pick up the pace. He didn't want to miss the monk's death.

◆ ◆ ◆

Angelica walked out of the tower only moments after Abraham and his reserves headed toward the battlefield. She started running as fast as her little legs would allow her. She had almost caught up to Abraham when she slipped on some bloody intestines left from the battle. Falling face first, she soaked herself in blood and guts, but worst, she severely twisted her ankle.

With blood dripping from her chin, the brave girl staggered to her feet and tried to walk, but the pain was too great. Hopping on one foot, she tried to move, but the bloody field made it nearly impossible, causing her to slip and fall again. Abraham reached the clash, and his reserves entered the battle, hacking away at the few remaining humans. Angelica tried to shout the Lord's Prayer as loud as possible, but nothing happened. They were too far away and couldn't hear her over the din of battle.

What do I do? Angelica could see her friends dying by the hundreds, and she was too far away to stop it. The young girl dropped to her knees, looked up into the heavens, and begged, "God, please help me."

The warm feeling entered her body. A fire from a thousand suns surged through her veins. A pure light beyond comprehension took hold of her soul and whispered the words she had never heard. She opened her mouth, and a roar came forth, shaking the earth, propelling her voice for miles.

"God the Father commands you.

God the Son commands you.

God the Holy Ghost commands you.

Christ, God's Word made flesh, commands you;

He who to save our race outdone through your envy, humbled Himself, becoming obedient even unto death;

He who has built His Church on the firm rock and declared that the gates of hell shall not prevail against Her, because He will dwell with Her all days even to the end of the world."

Nearly a thousand demons still remained as Angelica's words penetrated their ears. All of them started to shake, a blank look of bewilderment on their faces. Then black specks began to float upward into the air, flaking off from the creatures' bodies, little by little, until millions covered the area. Then instantly every demon disintegrated into nothingness.

"Ashes to Ashes, Dust to Dust," Angelica quietly mumbled.

Abraham was alone on the battlefield, only a hundred yards from Seng Shan, Katie, and ten other humans who had survived the battle. With an amazed look on his face, he fearfully stared at Angelica. Then he quickly looked at Seng Shan and saw the returning stare of vengeance. He turned his horse, laid his spurs into the animal, and took off back toward the tower as fast as his steed could run.

The survivors stood there for a few seconds, looking at

the little girl covered in blood in awe. They didn't know what to make of her and were prepared for the worst until Katie said, "That's my friend Angelica."

With Katie in the lead, the survivors crossed the distance until they reached the blood-soaked girl. Katie embraced her tightly and said, "I'm so glad you're okay." Then she pulled back, and with a perplexed look asked, "How did you do that?"

"I don't know, but that doesn't matter now. I can't walk. Someone needs to carry me to the tower before it's too late."

◆ ◆ ◆

The Master sidestepped and easily deflected the knife thrust. At the same time, he used his momentum, spun, and swung a back fist attack at my dark friend. My companion anticipated the strike and used his free hand to make an Eagle-Claw catch on the Master's wrist. Instantly, my warrior friend pulled the knife thrust back and in, aiming for the Master's jugular, but it was too late. Before my dark friend could land the strike, the Master ducked and rolled away, breaking away from my friend's grip. The Master was up immediately with a broad smile on his face, rubbing out the pain in his wrist, where the flesh had been torn away.

"Impressive," he said.

"I'm just getting started," responded my companion.

"It would be such a waste to kill you."

"It would be such a waste to keep you alive," answered my dark friend as he charged forward once again.

Admiration filled my heart as I watched him move, his blade hand weaving in and out, sometimes lunging in so quick, it was impossible to see. At other times, I could barely see upward and sideways slices. If these had landed, they would undoubtedly have caused immediate death. Yet, no matter how skilled my incredible friend was, it seemed the Master could avoid and counter every strike.

After a while, it seemed like the two warriors were slowing down, and I began to see every movement clearly, but then strangely, I realized they weren't moving slower. Everything else was. It was like some kind of lucid dream that I was stuck in. Not only could I see each movement, but I could understand every technique. I don't know what magic had befallen me, but I didn't have time to think about it now.

Then the Master went on the offensive in a furious display of skill. A high, spinning hook kick just missed my friend as he dipped his head backward. However, I could see he anticipated the strike and saw the opening, just before the Master's leg returned to the ground. He deflected an arm and lunged into the gap, his blade stabbing out hard.

But the Master moved beautifully, continuing his momentum from the spinning kick, at the same time dropping down low to avoid my friend's attack. The same leg he had spun high, now spun low as he pivoted on the ball of his foot, in a crouched position, and unleashed the sweep, like a tornado, toward my friend's front leg.

Yet, my friend is no fool to be so easily compromised. The sweep couldn't be avoided, so he accepted it, but at the same time, twisted his body in the opposite direction, letting the momentum of the Master's leg spin him into an aerial cartwheel and land harmlessly on his feet a few steps away.

Then it was my friend's turn to initiate the attack once again. He sent a front kick toward his opponent's groin, but this was only a fake, immediately followed up by a knife thrust to the chest. The Master didn't fall for the ploy and easily deflected both strikes, but the aggressiveness of the second attack, forced the Master to sidestep and move much closer to my companion.

This was my friend's plan all along, and as the Master moved closer into range, my friend attacked with his opposite hand. The Eagle-Claw catch zoomed forward at lightning speed, thumb and fingers hardened like steel from years of conditioning, snapping closed like a bear trap toward the Master's jugular vein.

But the Master was no novice to fighting in hand-to-hand combat. His uncanny speed was a blur, and where the exposed jugular should have been, turned into air in an instant. The Eagle-Claw fingertips barely grazed him, leaving a small bruise on his neck.

This mind-boggling exhibit of the martial arts went on for several minutes, each taking turns offensively, but neither of them gaining an advantage. Finally, they stopped and slowly circled each other. The sweat rolled down their faces like a leaky faucet that can't be turned off. The drips turned to puddles on the floor, making their steps treacherous. Their chests rose, mouths open, sucking the oxygen in and out, trying to regain their equanimity.

"You can't win. You'll fail once again like you failed your friends and family," the Master slurred between breaths.

"You're breathing heavy demon, much heavier than I am." My friend said clearly, as he moved in to renew the attack.

He was right. The Master was starting to falter.

◆ ◆ ◆

One of Seng Shan's warriors picked up Angelica and sprinted to the tower, followed by the monk, Katie, and the other survivors. As they entered the building, they came face to face with Abraham standing in the center of the lobby. His left arm was around Fu's chest, while his right arm pressed a knife against the young boy's throat. The demon he had sent to retrieve the boy stood at his side, sword in hand.

"Drop your weapons, or I'll slit his throat!" Abraham demanded.

The monk's face twitched with anger, undecided on what to do. He looked at his grandson, grappling with his decision, but emotions overwhelmed his judgment.

"Everyone put your weapons down," he told the group.

Reluctantly, Katie and the rest of the group dropped their weapons. Seng Shan was last and was just about to comply when Abraham pointed at Angelica and shouted, "No, I have a better idea. Kill that witch, and I'll let your grandson live!"

The monk stood motionless, so Abraham slightly dug the dagger into Fu's throat, causing him to scream as blood trickled down his shirt. Abraham shouted again, "Do it now!"

What no one realized, is the instant they had entered the lobby, Angelica had already engaged the enemy. She reached out with her specter-like powers and entered the mind of the demon standing next to Abraham.

Previously, the young girl had tried to control a demon and had failed. *I won't fail this time.* Angelica planted the images of the demons dying on the battlefield into the creature's mind. *You'll suffer the same fate if you don't obey me.* Quietly, the girl sent prayers at the monster. They weren't forceful but teasingly inflicted slight pain, letting him know how easily she could turn up the volume. The beast tried to fight the intrusion.

◆ ◆ ◆

Abraham heard the gurgling sounds to his right, so he turned and saw the demon struggling with some dilemma. The creature was shaking nervously, and drool dripped from its mouth. It snuck side glances at Abraham, avoiding making eye contact. Abraham looked at Angelica and realized his mistake. In that last second, an image of his brother Ray appeared in his mind, and he questioned himself, *Was I wrong?* Then the demon shoved its sword through his head.

The knife dropped from Abraham's dead hand as he crumbled to the floor. The demon just stood there in a state of confusion until Seng Shan quickly crossed the floor and cut off its head. Then the monk swept up his grandson and squeezed him ardently, tears of joy running down both of their faces.

Katie turned to Angelica and asked, "Where do we go now?"

"We're already here. Put me down."

Gently, they helped Angelica kneel on the floor, avoiding putting pressure on her injured ankle. She started to pray...

◆ ◆ ◆

They moved in and out, punches and kicks moving at lightning speed. Most of the strikes were blocked, but I saw a few of my friend's attacks find their mark. The Master was starting to tire, and the smile he once flaunted had turned to a grimace of fear.

The Master retreated and jumped over the dining room table. My friend tried to pursue, but the Master kept moving around, using the table to keep him at bay while he tried to regain his composure.

"I can see your thoughts. --- I know what you did," the Master said in between breaths. "You try to hide it away, pretending it wasn't your fault, but I see what happened. My demons tore your wife and daughter apart." A slight pause ensued, and then he pointed his finger at my friend accusingly and said, "Yet you were too slow to stop it."

"Shut up!" my friend screamed.

"Don't listen!" I yelled, but I felt the guilt gnaw at me. Memories long lost entered my mind and ripped at my soul.

"All the years of training, but you weren't good enough to save them," the Master stated with disgust.

"No!" I screamed at the top of my lungs as I fell to my

knees, tears pouring from my eyes like Noah's flood.

The Master sauntered around the table, slowly walking toward me. In a soothing voice, he said, "It's okay to cry. Yes, you failed them, but it's the false God that failed you. Why didn't he save them? Why did he allow them to die? I would have given you the strength to save them. I can guarantee that you will never feel this pain again. --- All you have to do is follow me."

Comfortingly, I felt his hand on my head. Looking up into his beautiful eyes, the painful memories melted away. In a trance, I saw my hand give him the knife.

Then the room vibrated violently as the energy of her voice penetrated the darkness. The Master screamed in agony as the words of exorcism were spoken...

"Thus, cursed dragon, and you, diabolical legions, we adjure you by the living God, by the true God, by the holy God, by the God who so loved the world that He gave up His only Son, that every soul believing in Him might not perish but have life everlasting; stop deceiving human creatures and pouring out to them the poison of eternal damnation; stop harming the Church and hindering her liberty. Begone, Satan, inventor, and master of all deceit, enemy of man's salvation."

The Master transformed before my eyes. A grotesque horned monster now appeared before me, his muscles bulging beneath leather skin, covered by a thousand open sores that oozed globs of phlegm. His face was pure horror, long and pointed with giant black eyes and a mouth filled with a hundred needle-like fangs.

Not only was the Master revealed to me, but now I could clearly see my surroundings. The ceiling and walls were gone. The tower was gone. Only the cracked concrete slab remained, littered with rubble. Nothing we had seen was real. My mind refocused, and the door closed, pushing out the memories of the past.

The monster was writhing in pain, covering its ears, trying to stop the holy words that Angelica was speaking. The dagger it had taken from my friend was in its hand, and I watched as it drew its arm back and launched the weapon at blazing speed toward Angelica.

Then something happened that I can't explain. One moment my friend was on his knees, the next he had instantly teleported in front of Angelica, then he was gone and behind the Master Demon. Grasping the creature by the skull, he jerked his body and twisted the creature's neck. I heard the resounding snap as the monster's neck broke, its lifeless body collapsing to the floor. My friend stood there for a second, his arms open wide, and then I saw the knife sticking out of his chest. He looked at me and smiled for the very first time, and then he fell to the ground.

The Last Chapter

Collapsing to the ground, I feel the sharp pain driving its way to my heart. My hands crawl up my stomach until I feel the wetness. Looking down, I see the hilt of a dagger protruding from my chest and wonder, how did this happen? My friend was the one that was stabbed, not me. My head tilts to the right, resting my cheek on the cold cement. Blinking my eyes, I search for my friend, but he is gone. Where did he go? How could he abandon me?

Angelica limps to my side and kneels next to me. She grasps my hand and brings it to her cheek, letting the tears roll over my fingertips and down the back of my hand. Why is she crying? She never cared about Bill and me before. She wouldn't even answer our questions, or did she? Confusion blurs my memories as doors open and close. Real life and dreams tangle and unwind. I try to focus, but reality eludes me.

Then Katie, Fu, and a monk dressed in orange robes also kneel next to me. The monk looks so familiar, and as I stare at him, the memories from my past flood back like a storm. I see myself as a child, and he is training me. The countless hours of blood, pain, and sweat run rampant through my brain. I remember his name. He is Seng Shan, and he was my Shifu. I was his greatest disciple and dedicated my life to his training. From the time I was a child until I entered the underground bomb shelter, he taught me everything he knew. In the end, I surpassed his greatest expectations.

This doesn't make any sense. Who am I? Then I see Bill, and while Angelica and the others bleed tears for me, he only laughs. I'm dying, and all he can do is laugh at me. Bill opens his mouth and says, "You pin-head! You still haven't figured it out." Then I see him start to vanish like that time earlier, but this time it's different. He starts to dissipate as he floats toward me, and I feel myself absorb him into my soul. The truth returns, and I remember he died many years ago in that car accident, but I also know he never left me.

Angelica squeezes my hand, and between sobs says, "Thank you. You don't have to fight any longer. You saved me and freed us all. It's time for you to go and be with them." She takes my journal from my pocket and says, "Don't worry, I'll finish it for you."

A path of light opens above me. It beckons me, and the goodness it exudes is irresistible. I choose the path, and my spirit floats upward. A surge roars through me as I enter, causing me to move faster than time or space. The bright lights overwhelm my senses, but I am not afraid. When my focus returns, I find myself standing in white mist. Everywhere I look, I see light, and all I can feel is happiness. A perpetual calm and peace wash over me, soothing my soul and massaging every fiber of my being.

Someone is running toward me, and then I realize it is not one being but two. As I step toward them, the blurred images come into focus. Joy takes hold of me, and my steps turn into a sprint. I move faster and faster until I see their smiles, and then I cover the distance in leaps and bounds. We come together, and I crush my wife and daughter into my arms. Rejoicing, I rain a thousand kisses upon them, and for the first time in so many years, I feel love. It all comes back, and I remember every detail. My mind clears, and for the first time in so many years, I remember who I am. I am HIM...

Coming Soon

And don't miss book 2 of the

I call him HIM

trilogy

The Angel of Death

By

Scott W. Kimak

Here's a special preview:

Prologue

"Look what you did," the voice whispered into the young boy's mind as he absorbed the gruesome scene in front of him.

"Don't turn your eyes away. Take a long look at what you did. Do you see the trail of blood? Follow it. Look at her intestines spread out across the ground. Look at her arms and legs stretched away from her body. Now, look at the man, or what's left of him. Look at his head lying over there on the ground. Look at his eyes. He's staring at you. He knows what you did. They were always so nice to you. How could you do this to them?"

"No!" the young boy screamed as the tears slithered past the red freckles on his cheeks. The recollections of what happened the day before needled their way to the back of his brain, as he stood there alone in the dust. He had to tell the demons which families in his village still believed in God. It was the only way he could protect his mother. If he hadn't told them, then they would have taken her away to the slave camp. He had already lost his father. He couldn't lose his mother too. He didn't want them to die, but he didn't want to be alone either. Is it such a horrible thing to want to be with your mother? It's not like he was the one that actually killed them.

"I had to do it! It was the only way I could save her!"

"So, you think you had no other choice?" the voice asked.

"No! It was the only thing I could do. I couldn't let them

take her. I saved her!"

After a brief pause, the voice quietly whispered, "Maybe you're right."

With great relief, the boy wiped the tears from his face and said, "Yes, I am right."

"Of course, you are. What else could you have done? You didn't have any control. It was your only option to stop them from taking her."

Enthusiastically, the boy nodded as he heard the words echo in his mind.

"Some might say that what you did took great courage," the voice whispered.

"Courage?" the boy quietly asked.

"Yes, I think you are very brave."

"Thank you."

"As a matter of fact, I think you're the bravest boy I ever met. You weren't afraid to tell them the truth, and that's exactly what you did. You told the truth. Why should you protect that dumb little girl and her belief in a false God? If this so-called God does exist, then why didn't he save her parents? If he does exist, then it was his fault they died, not yours."

"You're right," the boy excitedly responded.

"Of course, I'm right," the voice exclaimed. "There is much that you can learn from me. I can help you, but I won't give my advice freely. If you want my help, then there is a price to pay."

With reluctance in his voice, the boy asked, "How much will it cost me?"

"Don't look so glum. Has anything in this life been given to you for free?"

"No."

"Then why would I give you my help for free?"

"I guess you're right. What do you want?"

The voice answered, "All I ask is your obedience. Is that so much to ask?"

"No, I guess not. I can do that. What do you want me to do?"

The voice responded with a knowing smile, "For now, all I want you to do is listen and wait."

And young Jimmy Mcgregor did what he was told...

Thank you for reading my book. Please leave a review on Amazon and Goodreads.

Also, follow me at...

bestfantasybooks95@yahoo.com

https://www.i-call-him-him.webnode.com

https://www.facebook.com/scott.kimak

https://twitter.com/ScottKimak

https://www.instagram.com/scottkimak

Made in the USA
Middletown, DE
09 April 2024

52701105R00116